Quickies – 6
A Black Lace erotic short-story collection

T0314663

Look out for our themed Wicked Words and Black Lace short-story collections:

Already Published: *Sex in the Office, Sex on Holiday, Sex in Uniform, Sex in the Kitchen, Sex on the Move, Sex and Music, Sex and Shopping, Sex in Public, Sex with Strangers, Paranormal Erotica*

Quickies – 6
A Black Lace erotic short-story collection

BLACK LACE

This book is a work of fiction. In real life, make sure you practise safe, sane and consensual sex.

4 6 8 10 9 7 5

First published in 2007 by
Black Lace,
Virgin Books,
an imprint of Ebury Publishing,
a Random House Group Company

Learning Procedures	© Hannah Brophy
Rocky Mountain Rendezvous	© Kimberly Dean
Are We There Yet?	© Portia Da Costa
Coffee Break	© Alison Tyler
Private Performance	© Mae Nixon
Beautiful Things	© Cal Jago

Typeset by SetSystems Limited, Saffron Walden, Essex

Printed and bound in Great Britain by Clays Ltd, Elcograf S.p.A.

All rights reserved. No part of this publication may be reproduced, stored in a retrieval system, or transmitted in any form or by any means, electronic, mechanical, photocopying, recording or otherwise, without the prior permission of the copyright owner.

The Random House Group Limited Reg. No. 954009

Addresses for companies within the Random House Group can be found at www.randomhouse.co.uk

A CIP catalogue record for this book is available from the British Library

MIX
Paper | Supporting responsible forestry
FSC® C018179
www.fsc.org

Penguin Books is committed to a sustainable future for our business, our readers and our planet. This book is made from Forest Stewardship Council™ certified paper.

All characters in this publication are fictitious and any resemblance to real persons, living or dead, is purely coincidental

ISBN 9780352341334

To buy books by your favourite authors and register for offers visit www.randomhouse.co.uk

Learning Procedures
Hannah Brophy

Kevin Stoddard fumed as the elevator jetted its way to the twenty-seventh floor. His secretary, Miss Darcy, had quit exactly four weeks ago. Since that time, HR had managed to find him three temporaries, each worse than the last. Salvation from the last empty-headed blonde had come from an unexpected out-of-town trip. He didn't have to see her or put up with her gum smacking for the last three days of last week.

So, what had HR done? Hired Miss Darcy's replacement the minute he was gone. And then let the incompetent temp train her. Last Thursday's email had informed him a new secretary would begin on Friday.

Of all the dunderhead moves: did HR understand nothing about hiring underlings? Starting a secretary on a day when the boss was out of town just set a bad example. The woman was here to work, but her first day had been spent goofing off, because he wasn't there to take charge and set the pace.

Also, and this really had him steamed, he was entitled to final approval of any new hires for him. Probably it hadn't helped that he had called the head of HR, Mrs Jacobs, a bumbling jackass to her face. But the giggling temp in week three had set his teeth on edge.

All this had rained down on his head simply because he refused to authorise a year-end bonus for Miss Darcy, to encourage her to work harder this year. Instead, the ingrate had found a better-paying job and quit with minimum notice.

Kevin scowled at his fellow workers as he made his way down the corridor to his large corner office. His colleagues scurried out of his way. He worked long and hard hours for that corner office; was it too much to expect that his staff would work hard, too?

As he rounded the corner, his pace slowed. Rising above a low file drawer were two very long, very shapely legs that ended at a charmingly curvy rear end. She wore a flared floral-print skirt, dark hose and three-inch heels. Very nice. Maybe HR had gotten something right.

He paused, momentarily enjoying the view, but then she straightened. Her back curved upwards until she reached her full height. Neon blue streaked her short dark hair. When she turned to face him, he noticed three earrings in her left eyebrow and at least six hoops in each ear plus a peacock feather that dropped from the lowest hole almost to her shoulders. The blue in the feather was an amazing match with the colour of her hair. Lord, have mercy.

This was a law office, not a strip club. What was HR thinking?

'Katie Carlson.' She offered her hand and automatically he shook it. 'Your new assistant.'

Blue hair? Facial piercing? Assistant?

'Miss Carlson, is it?' He hastily dropped her hand. 'I need to make a call, then we'll talk about what needs to be done.' What had those idiots in HR done to him this time?

Impatiently, he dialled Mrs Jacobs' extension.

'Hello, Kevin. I thought I'd be hearing from you this morning.' Mrs Jacobs' cheery voice greeted him. The fact that he hadn't had to introduce himself reminded him of how much he disliked caller-ID.

Each time Mrs Jacobs called him by his given name, his stomach rolled. How many times had he told her he preferred to be called Mr Stoddard? Mrs Jacobs would nod and then answer with something like, 'Of course, Kevin.' And go on with whatever point she was attempting to make.

'I just met my new secretary,' Kevin announced, preparing to launch into his diatribe.

'It's the twenty-first century, Kevin. They are called assistants now.'

'Never mind that. Did you actually look at the girl before you hired her? She's fifteen and has blue hair!'

'Twenty-one, not fifteen, and the colour of her hair, I believe, is referred to as indigo.'

'I. Do. Not. Want. A. Secretary. With. Indigo. Hair. Do I make myself understood?'

'I'm not deaf and neither, I'm betting, is she. Miss Carlson has the best credentials I've ever seen. She should please even your impossible standards. Plus she already thinks of you as her grandfather.'

'Her grandfather? I'm forty-three, not eighty-three.'

'Really? Well, I mentioned that you preferred to

have your *assistant* read her work to you when you were tired. Apparently, she did the same for her grandfather. If you run this one off, Kev, you're on your own.'

Kevin slammed down the phone and paced the area behind his desk trying to regain his equilibrium. His mind raced. This would make him the laughing stock of the office. But if he fired her, he would be stuck with incompetent temps who couldn't even file, much less type. No, he had to make the best of this, until he could find the secretary he wanted.

'Miss Carlson –' he spoke through the intercom '– please come in.'

Katie Carlson entered the office and placed a cup of hot coffee on his desk. She did not sit, but rather stood to the right of his desk in front of the floor-to-ceiling windows. The daylight behind her highlighted her sheer skirt from the rear, allowing him to see the details of her slender thighs.

For a brief moment, he lost track of his train of thought. He took a sip of coffee to discover it was exactly as he liked it – one sugar, extra hot.

'You've come at a bad time. I've four weeks' worth of typing that hasn't been done, so we may have to work evenings to get caught up.'

Katie nodded and shifted her stance, but, as she did so, her pen dropped and she turned to pick it up. Kevin found himself mesmerised by the shadowy portrait of her round buttocks.

He realised she was speaking. 'What?'

'I asked, which files are most important?'

'That stack over there.' He gestured towards the

empty credenza. 'Shit! Someone's reorganised my office; I'll never find anything.' But, as he looked around the room, he realised it was neater than he ever left it. This was a disaster in the making.

'Done.' She moved to the credenza, opened the doors, removed a large stack of files and placed them on his desk.

'Done? What do you mean done?' he asked, relieved that his work hadn't been lost, but near hysterical that someone had worked on his files without his supervision. 'No one is supposed to touch anything unless I tell them.'

The look she gave him strongly indicated what she thought of that. He scowled at her and flipped open the first file trying to ascertain how much work it would take to correct her mistakes.

Katie stood next to him, close enough for him to smell her sweetness. His lower body twitched. He must need a woman badly if a waif with blue hair could turn him on.

Katie removed each file as he finished. Unless asked directly, she said nothing. He flipped through the file and found neatly typed documents. Begrudgingly, he was impressed. He flipped to the front and noted that she had painstakingly detailed the work that had been done. Her clear notes enabled him to see what needed to happen next.

Stunned, he sifted through file after file. Of course, he hadn't read her work yet, and that would probably be disappointing. But she was amazingly bright and well organised. Maybe he could convince her to part with the blue hair and earrings, even if just the ones in her eyebrow.

'You've done this before, haven't you?' he finally asked.

'Yeah.'

Quite the little conversationalist. He watched her profile as she worked her way through the files. Her puffy scarlet lips and large blue eyes were really quite attractive.

Her skirt draped over his knee allowing his leg to touch hers. Even through his trousers, it aroused him. Carefully, his hand slipped under her skirt and hugged her knee closer to him as though she might try to escape otherwise.

He watched for a reaction in her face and was disappointed not to see her expression change. However, he felt her widen her stance. Was it for better balance or to give him better access?

'Tell me about yourself, Miss Carlson,' he invited when the stack was complete.

'What'd you wanna know?' she asked, briefly reminding him of her age and the gum-smacking temp. Automatically, he released her knee and sat back in his chair, attempting to put some space between them.

'What did you do before?'

She turned towards him and stepped over his legs so that she straddled him from above. Her cute little ass rested on his desk. Had any other person in his office tried this, he would have yelled at them. She acted like they were best buds rather than employer–employee. 'Best buds' was a status he sought with no one – and particularly not with one of his employees.

Instead of mentioning his objections, he

remained silent, more fascinated with the way her skirt had stretched across her spread thighs and the hem had risen a few inches above her knees.

'I worked for another lawyer.'

'Here?' The conversation no longer held his interest. All he wanted was to place his hands under her skirt and push it up to her waist. He saw himself ripping off her pantyhose and panties and burying his head between her legs. He wanted to kiss her thighs and stomach and part the dark hair between her legs to delve deeply with his tongue . . .

'No,' she said.

'No what?'

'No, it wasn't here.'

'Where?' He prodded, trying to focus on her words. Getting information out of her was like pulling teeth, but he'd long stopped paying attention to her face; his attention was transfixed on her wide-spread legs.

'Why do you care as long as I do my job well?' she cheekily asked in a whisper. The atmosphere between them had changed so much that he didn't even bother to respond to her insubordination.

A bead of sweat had gathered across his upper lip. 'You have cute knees,' he said, as though that would justify his staring.

'Naw. They're too banged up from when I was a tomboy. The stockings hide it.'

So saying, she raised her leg high enough for him to catch a glimpse of white silk and she pulled an elastic-topped, thigh-high stocking down her leg to show him her scarred knees.

'Uh huh.' He studied her knees as she pointed out

scars and then hopped off the desk to pull up her stocking.

'You don't wear pantyhose?'

'Too confining. My thighs like to breathe. It's late. Your mail from last week is in the right-hand drawer. I've typing to finish. If you need anything else, let me know.' Without another word, she disappeared through the doorway, carefully closing it behind her.

Kevin needed a cold shower. He needed not to think about her thigh-high stockings, her white underwear and her freedom-loving thighs. The little minx was trying to keep her job by seducing him.

Kevin's appointments kept him busy the rest of the day and well into the evening. Miss Carlson's efficiency put Miss Darcy to shame. He saw her briefly each time she popped unannounced into his office: with more coffee and a ham-and-cheese sandwich at lunchtime or returning finished files and picking up others that needed attention.

He worked late. By the time he was ready to leave, the office had been empty for hours.

Her workstation reflected her neatness and organisation. He stood at her chair for several moments secretly inhaling her lingering scent. It reminded him of the earthiness of a spring garden after a downpour.

He shook his head to clear it of unwanted thoughts. If this was the direction his mind was going, he needed to get laid tonight. Obviously, he couldn't work around her if he was just going to be horny all the time. Right now, his prick was hard enough to hammer nails.

The Beamer took corners easily as it slid into the late-evening traffic. He dialled as he drove.

'Hello,' a soft voice answered.

'Hi, sweet cheeks. How've you been?' he asked.

'Kevin, you bastard! I haven't heard from you in weeks.'

'Now, honey, I've been out of town a lot with work. Did you miss me?'

There was a brief hesitancy, before the soft voice responded, 'You know I did.'

He laughed silently to himself. Oh, yeah! She missed him. Ten to one she was seeing a dozen other guys.

'Listen, baby, I need to come by and see you. I can be there in ten minutes.'

'Kevin, I'm already dressed to go out. Tonight's the opening at La Carimba.'

'I heard about it. But nothing happens before ten o'clock at one of those places. I won't stay long. I just really need to see you. It's been too long, ya know?'

A long silence followed, before she finally spoke. 'Yeah, I know. Come on by. I'll leave the door unlocked.'

Kevin slipped into Julianne's apartment and was pleased to see that she had left the light on in the bedroom. Julianne was a woman who understood his needs.

She greeted him sitting in the middle of her bed, wearing a low-cut purple teddy.

'Wow! You look hot,' he said as he pulled off his jacket and tie.

'Thanks. Now, just what is it that you needed to see me about? Tell me, what couldn't wait even one more day?' she teased him. Raising herself to her knees, she lowered the straps of her teddy slowly to her waist.

'Oh, baby,' Kevin groaned as he discarded the last of his clothes. 'Suck me. My dick's thought about nothing but your luscious lips all day long.'

Julianne laughed and rolled to the edge of the bed. Her long tongue darted out of her mouth as she leaned over, and her hand closed around his painfully erect shaft and stroked up and down before she gently tasted the head.

Kevin moaned, braced his legs against the bed and arched his body towards her. Normally, he loved to watch, seeing soft, feminine pink lips cover his cock, enclosing it entirely as it slowly began to disappear from view. It was a sight he couldn't see often enough, particularly with a talented woman like Julianne, who would take him deep and hold him there while her tongue and tonsils did the work. Looking down on curly blonde hair bobbing over him made him hard. It made him hard just thinking about it.

But tonight, when he closed his eyes, the lips that covered him were the scarlet ones that had haunted him all day long, and the hair that bobbed was dark with bright-blue streaks.

Unable to stand it any longer, he called out,

'That's it, baby, take me deep. Oh, Jesus, that feels good.'

He felt like a machine gun firing rounds when he finally came, but it did nothing to bring him the sense of completion he needed. Nothing seemed to rid him of his pesky little fantasies about his new secretary.

Julianne languidly stretched back on the bed looking like a cat in the sun, supremely pleased with her performance. Her teddy still hung at her waist; her firm breasts and taut rosy nipples were bared for his view.

'Lift up,' he encouraged, as he pulled the teddy from her hips and down her legs.

'I thought you weren't staying long,' she chided.

'I'm not, but you didn't think I'd just leave and not tend to you, did you?'

Julianne giggled again.

'Turn over, baby. Put these under you.'

She rolled onto her stomach using the pillows he handed her to elevate her hips. His fingers trailed down her back, followed by his tongue. Her buttocks tightened as his hands and tongue continued their exploration. She squealed when he bit her fleshy cheek, but relaxed her muscles, giving him access to the area he sought.

Her little brown rosebud twinkled and teased him, sparkling in the light from his tongue's juices. Julianne moaned pitifully into the tangled covers of the duvet.

From the nightstand, Kevin grabbed a tube of lip balm and spread it on the shiny head of his erect penis, giving a final squirt to his thumb.

'We're not going to go there,' Julianne protested and squirmed as his thumb began to massage the lubricant into her reluctant opening.

'Yeah, we are.' Kevin's hand pressed against the small of her back, holding her firmly in place.

Julianne attempted to clutch her buttock cheeks together but, with his thighs wedged between hers, she was wide open.

'You can do this the hard way or the easy way, baby. It makes no difference to me. I like both,' he admonished.

'I hate you when you're like this,' she squealed, although her voice remained muffled in the covers.

'Sure you do.'

He removed his thumb and began to push and press his slick cock into her. Finally, her defences gave way and her body opened to him. The plump head caused her to thrash beneath him, but Kevin didn't hesitate. His hand snaked between her body and the pillows and pressed hard against her mons.

'C'mon, sweet cheeks, just a little more. That's it. Take me all. Oh, that's real good, baby.'

One of his fingers slipped further under her and began to stroke her clit. Without warning she went up like a flashpoint. The woman who had just complained about how much she hated it became a little firecracker in the bed. It was all he could do to hang on for the ride.

Kevin actually whistled in the elevator the next morning. It wasn't like he'd be heard; none of the rest of the staff would show up for at least another 45 minutes. The office was empty.

Today, the training of Miss Carlson would begin. It was time to take her through her paces. An image of a naked Katie trotting around a corral, controlled by a bridle in her teeth and a whip in his hand made him smile. Today, her position in the firm would be made clear to her. She would learn to perform like the trained pony she would become. Keep those knees high, Miss Carlson.

Katie arrived precisely on time. His door remained open, giving him an unhindered view of her workstation. If she was aware of him, she gave no indication. He watched her struggle out of her lightweight coat and bend over to put her purse in her bottom desk drawer.

Today she wore a black suit with a short skirt and waist-length jacket. His phone rang as she momentarily disappeared from view. He was still talking when she returned with his coffee and papers, entering his office without his permission.

First things first – this girl needed discipline; she thought she could run all over him. He hung up the phone and barked at her, 'Don't come into my office without my sending for you.'

She set his coffee on the desk and continued just as if he hadn't spoken. 'Here's your schedule for today and yesterday's mail,' she said nonchalantly, placing them in front of him.

'What else?' he growled, realising her hands were still full.

'Stuff for your signature.' She stepped behind the desk and stood next to him, putting the stack of paperwork in front of him. 'Sign here.' She pointed a manicured nail at a line on the paper.

'Not without reading it.'

'Fine, read it. I'll come back.'

'No, if I have questions, I'll want you here to answer them.'

She sighed and shifted her weight on the balls of her feet − not once, but twice.

'What're you so fidgety about?' he enquired.

'It's so hot in here. The sunshine warms this room up first.'

'Take your jacket off, but you're staying till we're finished.'

'Whatever.' She removed her jacket. Her black blouse was completely sheer. Her translucent skin and every detail of her lacy, black bra, including the tiny pink bow that nestled between her 'C' cups, was readily apparent. The only thing that prohibited his view was the pattern of random white dots decorating the material. She tossed her jacket to a chair and bent over the paperwork.

Her scent was as he remembered − earthy, sultry and somewhat musky. He slid his chair back so he could once again look at her sweet ass. A vision of his cock being eaten up as it slid into her tight little bottom hole engulfed him.

'What're you doing?' She turned her head to look at him.

'Nothing,' he replied harshly, pushing his chair back under the desk.

He read the papers quickly. Her work was good, surprisingly so. Before he had finished signing, the phone rang. It was starting out to be one of those mornings.

Mr Lawrence, the senior partner, wished to see

him. The meeting stretched into lunch and beyond, complicating his day. By the time he returned to his office, it was after five and everyone had left.

Between appointments and court appearances, he had very little free time. Training Miss Carlson was turning out to be a challenge – particularly since she appeared to be doing the superior job of keeping *him* tethered on the leash. He'd given up trying to get her to enter his office only at his specific instruction and to only do the work he authorised. In a week's time, she had not only caught up his work, she was also now helping other secretaries – making him look like he didn't generate enough work to merit having a secretary. If left alone, Miss Carlson would be running the entire law office within a week and the nation within the month.

On Monday, she wore a shirt with a top that didn't quite meet at the waist. Her belly-button ring caught the light as she put down his morning mail.

'Do you have any other locations pierced that we haven't seen yet?' he demanded, knowing full well it was none of his business.

'Yes.'

'Where?' He wasn't really sure he wanted to know. And yet he hated that he couldn't resist asking.

She just smiled, more of a smirk, really, as she left his office. She was killing him.

Tuesday afternoon was hell on earth. A run in Miss Carlson's stocking was detected shortly after lunch. Instead of using the ladies' room, she opted to change at her desk. Through the open door he watched the ruined stocking being rolled down her incredibly long leg at a leisurely pace then carefully removed from her foot.

Just before it hit the trash, she changed her mind. For several excruciating moments, she played around, using the stocking to bind her hands both in front of her body and behind, tempting him with visions of bondage. Lovers' games he wouldn't mind playing with her.

Finally, she became bored and disposed of the old stocking in favour of a new one. Her toes were pointed as she placed the new stocking over them, gradually covered the arched foot and pulled it agonisingly slowly up her long leg, higher and higher, until heaven was only a few scant inches away.

Her phone rang, interrupting her final adjustments. She spoke for a brief moment before hurrying off. Kevin sat back in his chair. Obviously, he wasn't going to get any work done this afternoon. Maybe he'd call Julianne again.

It was too early for her to be home. Conjuring up lurid images of Julianne wasn't working for him. No, it was time to put a stop to his lusting after Miss Carlson. But how to go about it?

Katie reappeared at her desk an hour later. He wanted to demand to know where she'd been, but he didn't really care. He called her into his office, and began: 'I want to drop some paperwork off at your house later tonight. I'll need it first thing in the morning and I won't get here until half-past nine.'

Katie blinked a couple of times before she nodded.

Apparently, he had finally hit upon something that was new to her. Good.

'Write down your address,' he instructed.

As usual, she spoke very little but did as he requested.

'You live out pretty far,' he commented as he studied the card she'd handed him. 'Do you live alone?'

'Uh-huh. I like privacy.' She shrugged carelessly.

'Good, so do I,' he said, thinking, Yes, I do, sweet thing, and we're going to need it tonight.

At 7.30, he pulled up in front of the old farmhouse. The upkeep on an old place like this must be awful, but the well-tended yard gave the house a tidy appearance.

He threw his suit jacket and tie on to the back seat of his car and strolled to the porch. The front door was open and a disembodied voice greeted him. 'I'm here. C'mon back.'

Winding his way down the narrow hallway he passed a bathroom and two bedrooms to reach a room at the far rear of the house. Daylight outside was fading; the house lights had yet to be turned on. The gloom gave him a moment's pause, but he pushed forwards ignoring the warning bells in his head.

'Are you back here?' he asked at the closed door.

'Yeah. I've got a surprise for you.' Her young voice sounded happy, an emotion he hadn't really associated with her.

A cruel smile curved his lips as he pushed on the

door. The room was completely dark. No lights, no windows. He stepped hesitantly into the interior.

'Hang on, I'll turn on the light,' her voice offered, giving him some relief.

A red light bathed the room like a photo lab, but, as his eyes adjusted, he realised photography was not the room's purpose.

Katie Carlson stepped out from behind a screen. Up until this moment, he had pegged her office appearance as relatively acceptable, even with the dreadful blue hair and assorted piercings. Now, he took a step back. Her wardrobe appeared to be cast-offs from the television show *Xena, Warrior Princess*.

Thick brown leather armbands, lace-up sandals and a sleeveless micro-mini leather dress gave her an Amazon-like appearance. Her height was not a factor, but her slicked-back hair and bizarre make-up enhanced her animal-like features. Dark lines resembling native tattoos swirled around her eyes. Jagged spikes radiated from the lines giving her a fierce, menacing appearance. The wicked, coiled whip attached to her waist implied she meant business.

He grinned. This was going to be even better than he'd anticipated. So, Miss Carlson had recognised his challenge and felt able to extend one of her own. As an unexplored fantasy unfolded in front of him, his cock jumped to attention.

What did she think she was? A little dominatrix in the making? Hardly. But he'd let her have her fun, and then they'd see who was the boss. For now he'd play along.

'Where do you want me, mistress?' he asked,

struggling to keep his sarcasm from being apparent. So sure was he of his status that he didn't even attempt to hide his rising erection.

'On your knees,' she commanded, pointing to a location in the centre of the room. Her voice surprised him with its authority.

From a far wall she detached a shiny metal chain. At the end of the heavy chain dangled fur-lined metal manacles, which dropped from the ceiling almost directly in front of him. She quickly secured his wrists, but the slack in the chain gave him complete access to every corner of the room. He snorted with derision. What good would chaining him do? He was still in control. Once he had her under his thumb, he would completely dominate her, both here and at work. Let her have her little fantasy.

But, before he was able to put his plan into action, Katie stepped away from his kneeling form and flipped a lever on the wall. The chain that secured Kevin slowly cranked upwards forcing him to rise to his feet to prevent his arms from being jerked out of their sockets. Soon he stood on his tiptoes, hanging by his hands from the ceiling.

Well, wasn't she just a little surprise. Her equipment was good, he'd give her that.

The door to the hallway opened behind him. Did she have company? Had he not been suspended so securely, he would have turned to see who had entered.

'I can't believe it took you ten days to get him here,' a strangely familiar female voice complained.

'Well, he was in court three days last week,' Katie responded tartly, defending herself.

Kevin swallowed hard as he realised why he knew the voice. Somehow this wasn't going quite the way he planned. But, despite his misgivings, his erection tightened painfully. Sweat beaded across his brow and under his arms.

Miss Carlson stepped behind him. Her voice purred menacingly in his ear, 'You remember Miss Darcy, don't you? Miss Darcy, who worked sixty hours a week for you last year, but wasn't quite good enough for a year-end bonus? It seems she has some unfinished business with you. I know you'll want to give her your absolute, undivided attention.'

Kevin turned his head, attempting to evaluate the situation. Over his shoulder he could barely make out Miss Darcy in the red haze of the room. Her untended blonde hair fell about her shoulders in a way that used to irritate him, but now he found strangely erotic. As usual her attention was not focused on him at all, but somewhere on the ground.

'Step around here, Liz. Kevin wants to see,' Miss Carlson directed.

Liz Darcy moved to face him while continuing to fidget with a strap at her waistband. Kevin's knowledge of sex toys, he discovered at that moment, was severely limited, but it didn't require an instructional video to know that not only was Miss Darcy wearing a strap-on dildo, but it was also probably the largest one available.

'Girls, you're making a mistake,' he cajoled using his best courtroom tone but, before he could continue, a ball gag was slipped into his mouth from behind. Miss Carlson's usual efficiency was not working to his advantage this time.

'Liz and I can handle this without your interference or direction,' she spat, every bit as cold as the most accomplished dominatrix.

It was the longest sentence he had ever heard her utter and, to his amazement, she wasn't finished yet.

'Since you're so fond of fucking your employees we thought you would enjoy a turn-about. You know, goose, gander and all that?' She playfully patted his ass in a manner that left little doubt as to their intentions.

Kevin groaned.

Katie Carlson reached around his body and began unbuttoning his shirt, pulling it from the confines of his slacks. While Liz Darcy stepped closer to the front of his body, the obscene dildo curved upwards, bobbing between them.

Looking into his eyes, Liz gave him a shy, flirtatious smile. Aside from the dildo, she wore an open chain-mail vest which allowed her pert breasts to play a lewd game of hide and seek as she bent to unfasten his belt.

Jesus, he'd never been this excited. If she touched him at all he'd probably come in his pants. She was careful, he noted, as she eased his zipper over his protruding cock – even more so with the elastic band of his jockeys. His penis sprang free to dance in the cool evening air, vulnerable to whatever ministrations these two minxes chose to perform on him. Miss Carlson tied his shirt around his shoulders, leaving him naked to his knees where his pants pooled like a toddler's during potty training.

His penis looked tiny compared to the latex phallus, and Liz Darcy, seeing him make the comparison, stroked hers proudly, flashing him a gloating smirk before continuing with her tasks. Removing neither his shoes nor his pants she tightened the belt securely to his calves, immobilising him still further.

Small, cool slick fingers began to massage his buttocks – dipping between the crack to thoroughly lubricate him while Liz busied herself by leaning forwards and running her tongue around his navel. His nipples were drawn into hard points and, when her tongue moved over them, an electrical shock ran through his body.

He closed his eyes and didn't open them again until he felt fingers on his buttock cheeks prising them apart. He stared down into Katie Carlson's determined expression and felt the penetration begin. His tight muscles gave way most unwillingly.

'Smile for the camera,' she trilled, a most smug inflection in her voice, and jerked her head in the direction of a tiny red light he had failed to notice. She laughed as she moved away.

Slowly the dildo filled him, stretched him, and sweet agony tore through him. Smooth, long strokes enabled the pain and pleasure to swirl together. He wasn't able to stand much of this torture. Despite the horror of the situation – that he was being penetrated in the ass and enjoying it – he was unable to help himself. He came, spewing his milky white essence in a graceful arc to land harshly against the wooden floor.

But the movement behind him did not end. On and on Liz Darcy rode him. Amazingly, he hardened again almost immediately. Soft fingers clasped him. He opened his eyes to see Katie's dark hair descend over his cock as her lips took the turgid shaft into her mouth. Oh yeah, this was better than any fantasy he'd ever had. After the ignominy of being buggered, he was going to get a treat after all. Maybe Katie Carlson wasn't as cruel as she'd made out.

Liz Darcy cried out in pleasure behind him and her movement came to a halt just as Katie withdrew her lips from his penis. Not now. Not now. His pleading, muffled by the gag, sounded pathetic even to his own ears. When had he ever had to beg?

The door behind him opened and closed. Listening to the silence, he realised both girls had left the room, forgetting a major piece of equipment. The dildo was still firmly lodged deep within him. He strained to expel it without success. Minutes turned into hours and time folded in on itself. Exhausted beyond belief, he eventually collapsed, letting the manacles support the entire weight of his body.

Light filtered through the open door. Shit. What time was it? His clothes were tangled around him and he lay on the hard wood floor. Every muscle groaned in protest as he struggled to move his arms to see his watch. Eight o'clock. He was going to be late for work.

Above his head the manacles drooped, taunting him in remembrance of the previous evening. His belt had been loosened and a pillow and blanket had been provided, but the girls were long gone.

He wondered if Katie Carlson would show up at work today. Either way it occurred to him that he needed to send flowers to Mrs Jacobs, the head of HR.

Hannah Brophy's story, *Learning Procedures*, appears in the Wicked Words collection *Sex in the Office*.

Rocky Mountain Rendezvous
Kimberly Dean

The sunset was gorgeous. Jenna relaxed into her lounger and shielded her eyes as the sun dipped low in the sky. At such a sharp angle, her sunglasses were practically useless. Still, she couldn't make herself look away. The sky was alive with streaks of oranges, purples and pinks. The remaining yellow rays bounced off the choppy surface of the lake, making it appear as if thousands of diamonds bobbed on the surface. She was tempted to reach out and grab one before they all disappeared.

Which would be soon.

She glanced at her watch for what had to be the hundredth time and sighed. 'Hurry up, Shane.'

Once the sun slipped behind the peaks that surrounded Indigo Lake, the sky would fade and the water would grow dark. If he didn't hurry, he was going to miss the whole thing. You couldn't see a sunset like this in the city. She knew, because the view from the dock was one of her favourites. She'd rented this cabin just so she could share it with him.

So where was he? She was starting to get worried. *And frustrated.*

She shifted on her lounger, glancing around timidly. She'd driven up here early to take advantage of the afternoon rays and, as always, tanning had made her horny. As inconspicuously as possible, she rubbed the toes of her right foot against her left shin, supposedly fighting an itch. And she was. Only it was higher. Much higher, and rubbing her legs together did nothing to ease her distress.

In vain, she ground her bottom harder against the cheap plastic chair.

Tanning always did this to her. She loved to strip down to a bikini. She adored feeling the sun's rays caress her curves, her dips, and whatever secret creases they could find. This afternoon had been no different. The skimpy cut of her new red bikini had let the sunshine touch her all over. Her skin was warm, oiled, and tanned to a golden brown. Her body radiated heat from the inside out, and a tiny pool of sweat had collected in her navel. She wiped it away. She didn't need it to remind her that she was slick all over.

Whistles from a boat of fishermen nearly an hour ago had left her that way.

You're going to regret it if you don't get here soon, lover boy, she thought. The sunset wasn't the only thing Shane was going to miss. Her body was humming. Much longer and she'd take care of things herself.

She glanced again at the horizon. She hoped he was at least on his way. The winding mountain roads could be difficult to follow after dark – if he wasn't lost already. Indigo Lake was only about an hour-and-a-half drive from Denver, but the turnoff was easy to miss. This was Shane's first visit. Once a person got away from the noise, lights, and traffic, it seemed like a different world.

That was precisely why she liked it so much.

'Well, poop.'

She didn't know what to do. Cell phone reception up here was iffy at best, and she'd already left three messages on his work phone; one to tell him she was leaving, another to tell him she'd made it safely, and a third to ask where he was. Besides, she knew he wasn't still at the office.

He couldn't be that stupid.

She frowned grumpily. His work habits were the reason she'd pushed for this getaway in the first place. Plain and simple, Shane worked too hard. She knew he was in the middle of a big project, but the hours he'd put in on it were ridiculous. She wasn't a high maintenance girlfriend, but she'd warned him he'd better start showing a little more attention. Or else.

Was it really that hard to buy her some flowers, candy, or maybe say ... *get his cute butt up to the lake so they could enjoy a weekend together*?

His cute, tight butt ... 'Mmm,' she murmured.

OK, so maybe she'd give him the benefit of the doubt. Besides, she wasn't in the mood to let anything spoil what had been a wonderful, relaxing day.

She swung her legs off the lounger and stood up. The diamonds had left the lake and it was starting to take on its indigo cast. She pushed her feet into her flip-flops, tied her sarong low on her waist, and grabbed her watered-down glass of lemonade. The wooden dock creaked as she walked back to the shoreline.

She pushed her sunglasses onto the top of her head as she headed across the grass to their rented cabin. Just the sight of it made her happy. The simple, one-roomed, log structure spoke of a simpler time, although she much appreciated the luxuries of electricity and indoor plumbing. She'd found this place when her company had held a business retreat. The main house hosted conferences, but it was these rustic out-of-the-way cabins that kept her coming back. Some had lake access, while others were tucked away in the pine trees that grew thick around the lake. With as warm as the weather had been, she'd chosen this one so she and Shane could take a dip in the lake if they wanted.

Apparently, it was going to have to be a moon-light swim.

Which, come to think of it, could be even more fun.

A devilish smile spread across her face. She couldn't help it. Being outdoors like this filled her with energy and made her feel adventurous. Besides, a little hanky panky in the lake would be the perfect way to deal with the after effects of her tanning session. She could still feel ripples running through her body. Each step she took made her sarong brush against her legs, and her nipples tightened in response. She bit her lower lip. Hanky panky was so much better with two.

The door to the cabin groaned as she opened it and stepped inside. She hesitated, though, when she heard the rumbling of a vehicle. She concentrated on the sound, but it wasn't Shane's BMW; that thing ran like a clock. She glanced across the room to the phone on the bedside table and saw the red light blinking. That was probably him, though. She set her glass down so quickly that lemonade sloshed onto the table. Wouldn't you know it? She'd been out there trashing his good name, and she'd missed his call.

She hurried to the phone, but the noise from the vehicle outside grew louder. She scowled as she accessed the message box. What was it with men and their big trucks? Did they need to compensate that badly? That din was going to scare away all of nature's little bunnies, squirrels and birds.

'Hey, sweetheart. It's me.'

She concentrated on the call, but the noise of the engine became louder and she had to plug her ear to hear.

'Please don't be mad. You know I hate to do this to you.'

Do what? Her eyes narrowed. Oh, he wouldn't dare. The vehicle outside rumbled like a freight train, and she turned her back on it. She needed to hear this.

'I've run into a bit of trouble getting out of here.'

Out of the office? She let out a feral growl. She was going to strangle him with her bare hands.

And maybe she'd practise on the redneck driving that monster truck!

'Zip it, would you?' She flipped back the curtain on the window as the crunch of tyres on gravel became louder. Was he intending to drive right over her cabin?

The light was getting dim, but relief spread through her when she recognised the vehicle. It was Shane – only he was in Shawn's 4X4.

Car trouble. She let out a laugh. Here she'd been ready to string him up and the poor boy had had car trouble.

A silly grin spread across her face. She knew that shouldn't make her happy, but it did. She hung up the phone and hurried out the back door. Shane was just stepping out of the big truck into the shadows beneath a pine tree. The hazy light didn't stop her from seeing the layer of mud on the monstrosity he drove. Her nose curled. For as much as his brother loved that truck, you'd think he'd wash it more often.

'Jenna, I'm sorry,' he called as he slammed the door shut. He rounded the truck, but came to a dead stop when he saw what she was wearing. 'Whoa. Damn. You look –'

She planted her hands on her hips to let him see his fill. His eyes nearly bugged out his head, and she stifled a laugh. Oh, she was going to have some fun with this. 'Better make it good.'

He looked at her dumbly. 'What?'

'I've been waiting for you all afternoon.' Teasingly, she ran her finger down her breastbone into her cleavage. 'You need make it up to me for being so late, mister.'

His gaze zeroed in on her breasts. '*I* need to make it up to you? Didn't you get a message?'

Jenna felt the hum return to her body. He was practically salivating. Still, he stood twenty feet away with his hands stuffed into the pockets of his well-worn jeans. Poor baby. He thought he was in trouble. She decided to turn up the heat.

'I was just listening to it as you pulled up, but it was a little hard to hear.' She quit toying with the string that held her bikini top together and pointed at the 4X4. 'Car trouble, I understand, but did you have to borrow that thing from your brother?'

His head turned slowly towards the truck. He waited a half-beat before turning a mischievous smile on her. A delicious shiver ran through her as he sauntered towards her. When he stood only a breath away, he cocked his head and looked over her lustily. 'I did if I wanted to get up here – and I did.'

Darn it, he'd turned the tables on her. He was the one who was supposed to be squirming. She tilted her head back to look up at him. 'I'm still waiting.'

Boldly he reached out and tweaked her nipple. 'You look sexy, sassy . . . and horny as hell.'

Oh, God. That tweak had shot right to her core. She couldn't take it any more. She lunged at him. 'You're right about that.'

'Ooof!' he said on a sharp exhale as he caught her.

She'd jumped right up into his arms, wrapping her arms and legs about him like vines. He was tall. She shimmied up further, loving the friction of his clothes against her nearly naked body, and covered his lips with a kiss. 'Apologise, slow poke – and be creative about it.'

His arms automatically came around her, and his roguish grin widened. 'Will a slow poke do?'

'What do you think?' She brushed her mouth

against his again. This time he was ready. The kiss he gave her was so sexy and intimate, her toes curled and her flip-flops smacked against her heels.

Damn, she should have lured him out here sooner. He was different out in the wild – tougher, almost brutish. He was wearing jeans, boots, and a T-shirt – not his normal business suit – and she liked it. A lot. His musky scent blended with the smell of pine in the air, and it made her feel a little untamed. She kissed the side of his neck and found his pulse pounding. 'I was worried, you know. I thought you were in a ditch somewhere or lost on the side of a mountain.'

'Get real. When have you known me to get lost?'

'Duh. Like every other week.'

'Oh . . . uh, yeah. Well, I'm here now.'

'Good thing.' She nuzzled the side of his neck. 'I've been tanning. You know what that does to me.'

His hips shifted against hers. 'I'm getting a good idea.'

He was holding onto her like he didn't ever want to let her go. His hands were stroking up and down her spine, across her bottom, and along her thighs. The skin-on-skin contact made arousal unfurl deep in her belly. She hadn't realised how much she'd needed his touch. 'You'd better hurry,' she whispered.

He went uncharacteristically quiet, but she could feel the hard press of his cock against her mound. Instinctively, she rocked against him. He groaned, and his fingers bit into her bottom.

'Baby, you tempt a man to do things he shouldn't,' he said tightly.

The soft words sent a thrill through her. 'Live dangerously, Kilkenny.'

She expected him to kiss her. To carry her into the cabin. To do something.

Instead, he did nothing. A muscle ticked wildly in his jaw, but it was the only movement he made. 'Are you sure?' he finally asked.

She glanced at his face. The heat in his eyes ... The strength in his touch ... 'Oh, yeah.'

That slow smile returned, and his eyes sparkled. He looked like a hungry wolf just thrown a piece of raw meat. She took a deep breath and felt her nipples brush hard against his chest. The fresh air, the darkness, his moodiness ... It added a new component to her lust, and she felt reckless.

'Find out how much,' she whispered, daring him.

His eyebrows lifted, but he didn't break the contact of their stare. As brash as she'd been, Jenna's nerves still went jittery when his hand slowly moved from her bottom to between her legs. He let out a grunt of frustration when he encountered her sarong. He gathered the material impatiently until he found his way underneath it. Yanking the crotch of her bikini bottoms aside, he sent his fingers searching. Her desire pulsed hot and hard when his callused fingers touched her.

'Damn,' he murmured as he stroked her intimately. Watching her face closely, he pushed into her. 'Slick, soft and welcoming.'

'Oh!' she gasped. He'd started with two thick fingers, but was already working in a third. The pinch made her entire body go on alert.

His eyelids became heavy. He crammed all three

fingers deep and let them curl like curious worms. 'You feel incredible.'

So did he.

'Shane,' she groaned. She let her hands cruise over his wide shoulders. 'Take me inside. Now!'

His eyes became clouded, but when he turned towards the cabin, he didn't head to the door. Instead, he pushed her right up against the hewn logs.

'Uh uh. My way,' he said. His gaze swept up and down her heated body. 'We do it right here. Aunaturel.'

'What? Wait!' she said, her breath catching. Recklessness was one thing; exhibitionism was another. At least in the water, nobody could see any ... hip action. Night had fallen, but the moon would be up soon. The other cabins weren't that far away. 'Somebody might see.'

'You wanted me to be creative.' He wiggled his eyebrows at her before pulling his fingers abruptly out of her. Those devious fingers started working on her bikini top.

Whooo. Whooo.

'There's an owl watching,' she hissed.

He laughed, and two quick tugs sent the twin triangles of fabric flying. Jenna self-consciously clapped her hands over her breasts. It left her with no defences when his hand slid suggestively down her belly to her bottoms. He only bothered with the tie at one side of her hip. The material dropped and swung limply back and forth between her legs. The open access was all he needed.

The moon rose behind him, casting light onto her

body, and she shivered. He was looking at her like he could devour her.

'Look at you.' He sighed. 'Drop dead fucking gorgeous.'

He reached for the zipper of his jeans, and she squirmed. This whole back-to-nature thing was a little much, but the naughtiness of it made her hotter than she'd felt under the afternoon sun. She glanced around to see who or what else might be watching, and her excitement peaked.

'Fucking gorgeous,' he whispered again, looking deep into her eyes.

A thrill rushed through her when she felt his broad tip bump against her. With one smooth thrust, he pushed all the way inside.

'Ohhh,' she groaned.

His jaw went slack, and his body shuddered. He took a moment, buried deep within her, but then pulled back and began thrusting frantically. Her body arched, and she clutched at his shoulders. He was slamming home with every thrust.

'Christ, you feel good,' he panted.

Jenna moaned. He felt better. Each thrust ground her butt against the logs of the cabin, but her sarong protected her delicate skin. The contrast, though, was enough to make her want to yell. So she did.

'Shane!'

He bucked harder, nailing her to the wall. Jenna could hardly stand the pleasure. It felt naughty, exhibitionistic, and so damn good. She clawed at his T-shirt until she found her way underneath it to smooth, hot skin.

'Look at me,' he growled as he kissed her again.

He lifted her legs higher around his waist. 'Give it to me, baby. Give it to me.'

She clutched at the strong muscles of his back. They were going at it like two wild animals, and he was enjoying it as much as she. Satisfaction had tightened his face until he looked fierce.

'I'm close,' she gasped, suddenly overwhelmed by the wild emotions bubbling inside her.

He grunted, thrust hard, and lodged himself deep.

She tightened around him, and he smothered her cry with a kiss. He bucked against her one last time, and Jenna felt him spurt inside her. His weight pressed heavily upon her, and she sagged against the cabin, limp and satiated.

It was a long time before she noticed the crickets chirping or the wind whistling through the pine trees around them. The moon had risen higher in the sky, illuminating their lovers' clench to anyone who might chance a look. An echoing *Whooo* told her that Mr Owl had stayed for the whole show. She didn't care.

She'd just had the best fuck of her life.

'That wasn't a slow poke,' she said breathlessly. Emotion suddenly swelled inside her chest. She liked this guy so much. They'd only been dating for three months, but he was smart, successful, and unbelievably hot. His work habits frustrated her, but now that she knew how to get his attention ... whew!

'Can we go inside now?' she asked, her lips brushing against his ear.

'Is there a bed in there?'

'King-sized.'

'Oh, yeah.' He carefully lifted his weight from her and gathered her into his arms. 'We're going to need that.'

Much later, Jenna watched Shane from that same well-used bed as he tinkered around with the fireplace. It was summer, but at such a high altitude the air cooled off quickly. Besides, the room just didn't seem complete without a fire crackling. She glanced around the cabin. It seemed so simple by today's standards: a bed in one corner with a bathroom off the back, the kitchen near the front door, and a nice big stone fireplace as a centrepiece. The thick, log walls and exposed rafters made the place seem cosy and private.

And privacy was important, considering some of the things they'd done together.

A blush caught her by surprise, and her gaze went right back to Shane. He was having trouble keeping the fire alive and had settled back on his haunches to watch that it didn't go out. Again.

It was his fourth try, and she couldn't help but laugh. 'Need some help?'

He threw her a look over his shoulder. 'Think you can do better, Sassy Pants?'

'Sassy Pants?' she sputtered. She rolled her eyes and flung back the covers.

'My mistake,' he said, his gaze locking onto her body. 'You're not wearing any pants.'

'Smart ass,' she huffed. She marched across the room to him, but was keenly aware of her nakedness. She couldn't help it. He was watching every sway and jiggle of her body.

She watched him right back. The flames in the fireplace had finally caught, and they illuminated him, the light licking against hard muscle and sinew. The pure masculine beauty brought her arousal back with a rush. He was stronger than he'd been. More muscular. She knew that Shawn had been dragging him away from the office to the gym, and the benefits were showing.

It was enough to make a red-blooded woman drool.

She bopped him on the shoulder as she kneeled in front of the fireplace beside him. 'Sassy Pants,' she muttered again. 'That brother of yours is a bad influence.'

He caught her before she could get comfortable and lifted her so she straddled him. The hair on his thighs bristled against the back of hers as she settled onto his lap. His strong arms came around her, and with a sigh, she leaned back against his chest.

'What do you have against Shawn?' he asked, his voice close to her ear.

'Shawn? Nothing.' She ran her hands back and forth across his forearms. This was nice, sitting so intimately in front of the fire. Tonight, they'd gotten back some of the closeness they'd lost in recent weeks. In fact, she felt closer to him than ever. She didn't want to spoil it with talk of his brother.

He cupped her breast and gently fondled her. 'Come on,' he coaxed. 'Tell me the truth. He seems to get you all riled up. It bothers me.'

Not as much as it bothered her. Shawn did get

her worked up, but in more ways than she wanted to admit. 'He's a pain,' she said simply.

That prompted a quick laugh out of Shane.

'Well, he is,' Jenna said. She glanced over her shoulder. 'He's always teasing me and playing practical jokes. He can never be serious.'

'Yes, he can. He just likes you. That's how he shows it.'

'By pestering me? What is he? Eight years old?'

Shane's hands caressed her intimately. Her nipple perked up under his attentions and poked into his palm. 'Definitely not eight,' he murmured.

Jenna let her hands run along his thighs. His touch was distracting her, but if he wanted to know her feelings for his brother, she was going to tell him. She was still miffed about a thing or two. 'That singing telegram he sent me at work was not funny.'

'Yes, it was. Admit it,' he said, giving her nipple a firm pinch. His tone changed. 'At least he remembered your birthday.'

Her breath caught at the sting. It only drove home the memory that Shane had forgotten. He'd been in Europe on business. 'Well, maybe it was a little funny,' she said, trying not to dwell on the issue.

'And thoughtful?'

'Don't push it.'

He hugged her more tightly and one hand trailed straight down her belly. His fingers brushed against her patch of dark hair before disappearing between her legs. She arched sensuously when he cupped her. 'He's crazy about you, Jenna. I'd like it if the two of you could get along.'

Her stomach dipped. With the way he was touching her, her thoughts went to a very naughty place.

'It would make me happy,' he said.

She nibbled on her lower lip nervously. He just wasn't going to let the issue go. She didn't want to cause a rift between the two of them, but she had to tell him the truth. 'I think it's a little more involved than that,' she said softly.

His hands hesitated, and he leaned over her shoulder so he could see her face.

She couldn't meet his eyes. 'Shawn wants me,' she finally whispered.

'And?'

And?

She looked at him, dumbstruck.

'He'd do anything for you, Jenna. Anything at all.'

Words stuck in her throat. What was he saying? Didn't he understand? His brother wanted her, his girlfriend, in a sexual way.

'Can't you give him a chance? For me?'

Her heart began to pound triple time. Shane understood just fine. It was she that was a little slow on the uptake.

Heat suddenly suffused her. The warmth of the fire was bombarding her, but it wasn't nearly as hot as the chest rubbing against her back or the hand stroking between her legs.

'You and Shawn would be really good together,' Shane said. He nudged her knees wider and static electricity jumped from the rug beneath them.

It seemed to shoot straight to Jenna's core, and she shuddered.

Wide-eyed, she looked at him. She peered into his dark eyes, and realised he was serious. Her thoughts whirled. She'd known the two brothers were close, but she'd never imagined this. What, exactly, were they into? The possibilities made her squirm in his arms, but yet, she didn't try to get away.

The muscles in his arms bunched as he adjusted her on his lap. Her thoughts were too chaotic to understand until he lined her up with his ready cock. She sank down and a sigh of pleasure left her lips. Oh, he was incorrigible.

'Just think about it,' he said as he began to rock their bodies together in a slow, sultry motion. 'For me.'

How could she think of anything else? She closed her eyes tightly, but that didn't stop her thoughts from running straight to the forbidden. Shawn did want her. She'd caught him looking at her many times, and he was a hottie in his own right. When he wasn't irritating her to death, she'd looked back – but she'd never let that on to Shane. She was a one-man woman, and she hadn't wanted to hurt him. Besides, looking was all she'd ever done.

But here he was, telling her she could do more. He wanted her to do a lot more.

Her fingers bit into his thighs. With each slow stroke, her thoughts bounced from one brother to the other. It made her feel wanton. Sexy. Desirable.

And totally out of control.

She tried to bounce more quickly on Shane's lap,

but he wouldn't let her. Using his strength over hers, he turned and settled her lengthwise onto the fur rug in front of the fireplace. 'Stretch out for me, baby. On your belly.'

Jenna let out a slow purr. She'd never been so stimulated in her life – physically, mentally, or emotionally. Not missing a stroke, he put her on her knees and she unfolded. She went down slowly until she was prone with her legs spread wide. His hand slid under her to tilt her hips back at just the right angle before he lowered his weight onto her.

'Mmm,' she murmured. She stared into the fire dreamily. Two sexy brothers. One hot night.

'Good?' he asked, his hips moving leisurely as he pumped in and out of her.

It was better than good, especially with the naughty things he'd said to her. It made everything seem more scandalous. Debauched. Illicit.

And maybe a little enticing?

Her fingers curled into the soft fur. It tickled her at all the right places. She closed her eyes and let herself sink into the feeling. 'Perfect.'

He was in no hurry. Together, their bodies undulated slowly. The fire crackled as the summer breeze blew outside. In the distance, Jenna heard her owl hoot.

'Who are you thinking about right now?' he whispered into her ear.

She didn't even think of lying. 'Shawn.' She sighed.

He pushed deep and ground against her. 'Good girl,' he said gruffly.

He dropped a kiss onto her temple, and her low moan filled the cabin. When the orgasm started, it was hot and pure. Where it ended and the next one began, she never knew. She came hard, and she came long.

And both Shane and Shawn were right there with her.

Sunlight woke Jenna the next morning. She groaned as she rolled away from the east-facing window. She'd forgotten to pull the shade.

Shane tucked her against him as she snuggled into his chest. 'Too early?' he asked, brushing her hair over her shoulder.

'Too bright.'

She shifted even closer, burying her face against his neck to blot out the sun's rays. Instinctively, she wrapped her arm about his chest and her leg around his waist. She came fully awake when she felt him bump up against her.

'Too sore?' His voice rumbled through her.

She groaned. She was, but she wasn't going to let that stop her. She let her tongue dart out to touch the pulse at his neck. When he shuddered, she pushed him onto his back and kissed her way up his jawline.

What a wonderful way to start the day. The fresh country air made her feel free, strong, and sexy. Her hand slid down his chest. She'd just found his cock when her stomach grumbled.

Beneath her, Shane let out a laugh. 'Ah, sweetheart. You need sustenance if we're going to keep this up for the next two days.'

Next two days? Lord help her.

She rolled off of him and pushed her tangled hair over her shoulder. 'There's food in the kitchen. I'll make something.'

'No, no,' he said, catching her by the shoulder and pressing her back against the mattress. 'You've been doing things for me all night. I'll run down to the bakery in town.'

Jenna sagged against the pillows. Something chocolate and gooey sounded perfect. With the way they were going, she'd burn off the calories before lunch. 'Wait,' she said, a thought occurring to her. 'Do you even know where the bakery is?'

'What? Oh yeah, I saw it on the drive up.' He threw her a cocky grin. 'I was hungry, but then I got here and someone distracted me.'

He kissed her before climbing off the bed to search for his jeans. He looked out the window as he pulled them on. 'God, what a sunrise,' he said, surprising her. 'We should go out for a hike later. Know any good trails?'

'Name your level. Wussy beginner or super stud mountaineer?'

'I think you know the answer to that.'

She rolled her head on the pillow towards him and smiled. It made her feel good that he wanted more out of her than just sex. She wanted to do everything with him: hike, bike, swim, and even talk. 'Did you get to see any of the sunset last night?'

He threw her a wink. 'It was nearly as gorgeous as you.'

She blushed.

'Try to get some more sleep,' he said as he

grabbed his keys. He dropped a quick kiss on her brow. 'I'll be back as soon as I can.'

'Mmm,' she said, already scrunching up her pillow. 'Drop some bread crumbs or something. If you get lost, I'm too tired to come find you.'

He gave her bottom a quick tap. 'Sassy pants.'

She grinned and watched him walk out the door, but noticed something on the floor behind him. She laughed when she realised what it was. He wouldn't get far without his wallet.

She pushed back the covers and walked over to pick it up. The well-worn leather flipped open when she lifted it, and his picture stared up from his driver's licence. She couldn't contain her curiosity. 6'2". 210 pounds. Brown eyes. Brown hair. Shawn Kilkenny.

Jenna froze. She looked again, but the name didn't change.

Shawn Kilkenny. *Shawn.*

Her brain stumbled, but then took off at a lightning pace. She spun around towards the fireplace. Oh, no. It couldn't be – but her nerves began to sing that it was.

That devil!

The phone caught her attention, and she lunged for it. Her hands shook so badly, though, it took her forever to get the message to play again.

'Hey, sweetheart. It's me.'

Her entire body jerked when she heard Shane's voice. It was different from the one she'd heard all night. Not much, but different enough to make her insides start to shake. Oh, God. How could she not have realised?

'Please don't be mad. You know I hate to do this to you. I've run into a bit of trouble getting out of here.' Shane's voice sounded distracted – as if making the call wasn't one of his priorities. 'One of our contractors just informed us that he's not going to meet his deadline. That means I have to make a bunch of calls and reschedule everything. Believe me, sweetheart, I'm just as upset about this as you are.'

Oh, really? Somehow Jenna doubted that.

The message continued. 'I know you'll understand, though. You're always so good about that. And hey, I just talked with Shawn. He was thinking about going fishing this weekend, so I told him where you are. He said he'd drop by and keep you company. Maybe you two could cook some s'mores or something.'

Cook some s'mores? Jenna let out a snort. He really was clueless, wasn't he? She slammed down the phone, unable to listen any longer. Her mind was abuzz. So she was 'always so good' about being stood up, was she? He hadn't even been listening to her!

A truck door slammed outside, and she twirled around. Suddenly, she found it hard to breathe. And him!

Shawn's little practical joke had gone way too far. She blushed when she remembered all the things they'd done together. And her naughty thoughts as they'd made love in front of the fireplace. She gasped. He hadn't been talking about a three-way. He'd just wanted her to be thinking about him.

The deviant!

But it had worked ... she hadn't been able to get him out of her head.

Her sense of indignation wavered. It was outrageous, but he'd pulled this stunt just to be with her. She was well aware that he'd been bird-dogging her ever since she and Shane had first hooked up. This wasn't a momentary fascination on his part.

It wasn't on hers, either. If she were honest with herself, she had to admit she wanted to be with him, too. If she'd met him first, she would have been all over him. He made her laugh, the sex was incredible, and he'd always been more attentive than Shane.

She was a one-man woman, but that didn't mean her man couldn't change.

She heard his footsteps start to come her way. She crossed her arms over her chest as she waited, but a smile pressed at her lips. Oh, this was going to be more fun than anything. She was ready and waiting when he opened the door. 'Hello, *Shawn*.'

He froze, one hand on the door handle. When he realised she was standing there buck naked, he quickly closed the door behind him. 'Easy now,' he said anxiously. 'Don't blow a cork. I never meant for this to happen. I got here and you just assumed ... hell, you're the one who jumped me.'

'You could have stopped me.'

'Are you insane?' The look on his face turned pleading. 'Oh, come on, Jenna. I'm mad about you. You've got to know that.'

'I do.'

'Just let me –' His head snapped back. 'What?'

'Oh, don't mistake me. You're going to pay, buddy boy. You're going to spend the rest of the weekend doing some very creative apologising.'

The worry on his face was swiftly replaced with a wicked grin. 'Anything you want, baby. Just say the word.'

'I want you.' She crooked her finger at him and smiled saucily. 'Get over here, you evil twin.'

Kimberly Dean is the author of the Cheek novel, *High School Reunion*. Her short story, *Rocky Mountain Rendezvous*, appears in the Wicked Words collection *Sex on Holiday*

Are We There Yet?

Portia Da Costa

'Where are we going?'

'It's a surprise.'

'Oh, go on. Tell me.'

'Don't be so impatient, wench.'

Wench? What is this? A sexy pirate fantasy? It's
Stone's clapped-out Toyota we're about to board, not
the fucking *Golden Hind*.

At least I *think* it's the Toyota. He doesn't usually
use the Merc for jaunts like this. But I can't be sure
because he's got me in a blindfold.

Yeah, I'm wrapped around in a world of pitch-
blackness, strung-out nerves and one man's per-
verse peccadillos. It's so exciting that I think I might
faint.

'Oof!'

I stumble on the gravel, and obscene messages
streak along those tight-strung nerves. For one
churning second, I have a horrific feeling that something totally disgusting is going to happen. But
luckily it subsides just as quickly and I'm back to
being weak and girly and clutching at his solid
muscular arm as he helps me with all courtesy into
the car.

'Are you all right, Miss Lewis?'

His voice is soft and genial as he settles me into my seat and fastens the belt across my chest. He has to do this because he's got me in handcuffs, too, as well as the blindfold. I'm totally vulnerable, but I can't deny that I like it.

'Yes, thank you, Mr Stone,' I answer, keeping it bright and pert and slightly insolent because that's the game we're playing tonight.

He murmurs, 'Hmm...' as if he suspects my motives, then softly slams the door and makes his way round to the driver's seat.

I know the blindfold is part of the game, but suddenly I wish with all my heart that I could see him as he settles in beside me and starts the engine. I want to see that dear profile of his. The solid, stubbly jaw. Those unexpectedly lush and overtly sexy lips. Long, long eyelashes that make me jealous as hell that it takes three coats of Maybelline to get the same effect. Taken overall, he's not exactly an oil painting but to me he's just sex on two long legs.

He revs the car and the vibrations of the engine play havoc with my insides because of the thing he inserted into me earlier. I hardly dare put a name to it, because it's not exactly the most refined and sophisticated of sex toys. But Mr Stone likes it – so that makes it fine by me.

OK, it's a butt plug, right?

And it provokes the rudest, most insidious of sensations. It feels like ... It feels like ... God, I just can't bring myself to say what it feels like. But at the same time, oh boy, it gets me going!

And Mr Stone knows that. Which is why he put it in me before we set out.

My mind flicks back to the bathroom and I start to sweat as if it were happening all over again. I'm naked, bending over, one foot on the edge of the bath. I'm totally exposed in the lewdest of ways and he's just looking, looking . . .

And then there's that sensation. Intrusion. Pushing. Pressure, pressure, pressure, then the give as it goes in. Oh, God! Then I'm exhibiting myself to my lover, slick and dripping, with that stark black rubber base protruding from my fundament.

It just boggles the mind what a girl will do for love.

As I zone back into the world of here and now, I wonder if he's deliberately searching out bumps and potholes. The old car trundles along, bouncing me around in a way that makes me gasp and gulp. The suspension leaves a lot to be desired, and so does my self-control tonight. But Mr Stone loves pushing my buttons and testing my limits.

One particularly juddering lurch has me biting my lip, and, though I can't see him, I know Mr Stone has noticed.

'Are we there yet?' I ask by way of a distraction. And he laughs.

'Impatient, Miss Lewis?'

'No.'

'Liar.'

'I just want to know when we're going to get there.'

'You might not be so keen if I told you.'

My heart kicks, and so does my sex.

Are we going dogging? We've done it before. And done it enough times for me to know that I'm just as much of an exhibitionist as he is.

I remember the first time, travelling there in this car, and it makes me sort of breathless.

I could see, that time, and Mr Stone gave me plenty to look at. And more. He asked me to take his dick out of his jeans and touch him.

Oh, my God, he might even have his dick out now for all I know!

I edge sideways, and begin to lean towards him. I may be handcuffed, but I can still reach over in search of our pride and joy. It's certainly big enough to find in the dark.

'What are you doing, Miss Lewis?'

'Um ... nothing. Really ...' I lie. 'Just trying to get comfortable.'

He says nothing, but I can sense that he's smiling. It's a slow, sly, sideways grin. I know it well and it slays me every time I see it. Even after all our months together.

Time seems to dilate and warp. I've no idea how long we've been travelling. I can measure it only in terms of what my body's telling me. The growing pressure in my belly. The growing wetness in my knickers. The way my clit aches and throbs and throbs and throbs. I want to ask if we're there yet again, but there's a pressure on my tongue too. The awareness of what might happen if I speak.

You might be wondering why I call him 'Mr Stone' when we live together.

Well, I don't a lot of the time. Mostly, he's just

'Stone', or maybe 'Robert'. And sometimes he's 'Bobby' when things are close and sweet and tender. But when we go all formal on each other it's a signal. Let the games commence. I only have to hear him say the words 'Miss Lewis' and I want to come.

'So, are we comfortable yet?'

His words make me jump and that plays havoc with my innards. I have to gasp for breath and gather myself before I can answer.

'Well, I don't know about you, but I'm just fine. Thank you.'

'Really? Is that a fact? I was just thinking that by now you might want to touch yourself.'

I've been wanting to touch myself since the bathroom, but I'm not going to tell him that. Instead I sneakily clench my thighs in an attempt to get some stimulation. It's a huge mistake though, and only makes things worse.

'Why on earth would you think that?' I pause, then add sassily, '*Mr Stone.*'

'Have a care, young lady,' he shoots back. More quickly, I suspect, than he intended. He puts on this act of total self-control. Impassive lack of interest in the sexual tension growing between us. But I know I'd be on a winner if I put good money on the fact that he's rampantly erect.

I get that yearning, burning urge to touch him again, and confirm my suspicions. I fancy that I could come from the simple act of touching his thigh. Which is bullshit, really, and I know it. This isn't some flowery, unrealistic romance here. Like any woman, I need my fair share of purposeful, inter-thigh fumbling to get me off. Fingering.

Tonguing. What have you. Or maybe a good hard shag? A bit of old-fashioned, tried and true, pneumatic grinding between the sheets with Mr Stone on top, his big size-eleven feet braced against the footboard so he can really put it to me.

Yum!

'What are you thinking about?'

Oh, shit! I realise that not only have I been quiet for several minutes, I've been jiggling about, trying to get some action by knocking that accursed butt plug against the root of my clit somehow.

'Nothing, Mr Stone. Still wondering where we're going and if we're anywhere near there yet.'

'Bullshit,' he observes roundly. 'You're thinking naughty thoughts, aren't you, Miss Lewis? If you aren't, I'll be surprised –' he pauses for a beat '– and disappointed.'

Oh, no!

'All right, all right, I was thinking about coming. And how much I want to do it. And all the ways I could do it.'

'That's more like it.' He starts to change gear and misses the one he wants. And I laugh out loud.

Touché, Clever Bobby, you're as horny as I am!

He treats me to one of the foulest, most disgusting oaths I've ever heard – all delivered in his most cultured and pleasantly conversational tone. Then, a moment later, he brings the Toyota to a halt.

Before I can ask if we actually are there yet, he's out of the car, round my side, and gently but determinedly hauling me out of my seat. He leads me a few steps away from the car, and simply says, 'Come, then.'

'H-here?' I stammer.

But where is 'here'?

I can hear the roar of traffic in the distance, so we must be near the motorway, but, other than that, we could be anywhere.

With anybody watching.

Not that that would bother me too much. It wouldn't be the first time I've put on a show. But still, not actually *knowing* whether there's an audience is unsettling.

I reach out my hands blindly in the dark, but I can find neither anything to sit on nor anything to lean against. And, goddamn him, he offers no assistance.

With a resigned sigh – and a great deal of difficulty, due to being cuffed – I yank up the hem of my skirt and fish about in my knickers.

'Tuck it up,' he instructs, 'and then pull down your pants to your knees.'

I feel faint again, and it's not from disorientation. My head goes light and I feel as if I'm floating on a cloud. Scrabbling and fumbling, and trying not to dislocate my shackled wrists in the process, I obey him. And display my crotch to the chilly night and its thousand eyes.

Remembering certain preferences of his, I spread my legs as much as I can with my knickers at half-mast. I know Mr Stone likes it when I lose my elegance. He likes it a lot. His dark side gets off on seeing me graceless.

I half crouch, half squat, and reach for my sex. It's like a swamp down there, and I'm so sensitised that I moan aloud. The erotic tension, the plug, the darkness. It's all brought me to fever pitch far too quickly. I touch my clit and feel a deep throb that seems to grab at the thing inside my bottom. The temptation to go for orgasm immediately is breath-taking, but I know that Mr Stone wants a perform-ance. So I withdraw from the most critical area and start to wiggle.

I must look a bit of a sight. Half crouched and waving my bum about. I drift into a strangely detached state, while inwardly watching both myself and the man who's watching me.

I suspect that he'll be masturbating too. That is if we're not in a public car park or a lay-by or some-where with dozens of folk around us. Maybe even if we are? I imagine those big hands on that big dick and I wish I knew exactly where he is in relation to my position. The ground beneath my shoes is soft, and, as Mr Stone is light on his feet, it's impossible to hear his tread. He hasn't spoken for a few min-utes either.

But I *should* be able to locate him. After all, he's six foot four and broad with it, and he displaces a lot of air. Yet I've no idea whether he's close by, or many yards away. If it weren't for the fact that I would've heard the engine start, he could have got back in the car and driven away.

And then I nearly faint when I feel his warm breath on the back of my neck.

'You're not trying very hard, are you, Miss Lewis?' he murmurs, so close he could be touching me. And in fact, a second later, he *is* touching me.

I feel his towering form against my back, his erection rampant as his arms come around me. One huge paw cups my breast, and the other swoops low to direct my masturbation.

His middle finger presses mine against my clit and I come like a runaway train!

My mind goes blank for a bit, but as I get myself together again, and realise I'm sagging against a still very insistent prick, I struggle with my cuffs and try to twist around to fondle him.

'Tut, tut! That's enough of that,' he says sternly, swirling his hips away from me while still holding my body aloft.

Even though my entire pelvis is still softly glowing with satisfaction, I feel disappointed. I so want to touch him. I so want to *see* him. I'd love to snatch off this stupid blindfold, reach for his amazing penis, and watch his broad face contort in pleasure as I caress him.

But it seems I'm not to get my wish, because, almost immediately, I'm being gently but firmly manhandled towards the Toyota with my skirt up and my knickers still at half-mast. I try to right them, but I get that 'tut, tut' again so shuffle along the best I can.

So, I'm to sit here with my bush hanging out, am I?

It seems that way, as Mr Stone restarts the engine.

How long have we been going now? How long have I been sitting here with my pants down and my skirt up? How many astonished fellow motorists have glanced idly to one side at the traffic lights – and got an eyeful?

It seems like an age, and it's not only my wandering mind that's telling me that, either. The cups of coffee I drank before we left the house are beginning to make their presence felt.

God, I need to pee! I really, really, really need to pee!

And it's all made worse by the nasty pressure of the butt plug. There just isn't room in my innards for a full bladder and a great, honking chunk of black rubber, too.

Around a dozen times, I consider surreptitiously clutching myself in a pathetic attempt to control the ache. But, even though he's driving, I know Mr Stone will be watching my every move. And even if he isn't actually looking he'll be monitoring me with his sixth sense. The one that can reach through the walls and corridors of the rambling, shambling Borough Hall building where we both work and tell at any given time whether I'm thinking or doing something naughty.

'Still comfortable?'

The bastard! He's read my mind – although it doesn't really require telepathic powers to deduce what sort of state I'm in. He was the one who offered me a second Americano.

'Fine. Are we there yet?'

'Not yet. Why, are you thirsty? There's a bottle of water in the glove box. Why not have a drink?'

Screw you!

'Well if you won't, I will. Can you get it for me?' he continues, his voice perfectly normal to the ear, although with *my* sixth sense I can hear him laughing his head off.

I refrain from pointing out that I can neither see nor use my hands all that efficiently, and just fumble around until I find the glove box catch.

The water sloshes as I pull out the plastic bottle and that does terrible things to my beleaguered bladder. This time I can't stop myself from wriggling, and twisting my thighs around, and Mr Stone notes that with a soft, impatient sigh.

I uncap the bottle and hand it to him, then have to sit there in a state of delicious agonising discomfort while he drinks deep, audibly relishing the cool water as it slides down his throat. With a grunt of satisfaction he hands me back the bottle.

'Sure you won't have some?'

'Absolutely.' My teeth are gritted but I get the word out.

We drive in silence a little longer, and again he seems to be navigating with the express purpose of seeking out the most dug-up and roughed-up bits of road. With every jounce and bounce of the car, I'm convinced I'm going to either cry out or wet myself or both, and eventually I just can't take it any more.

'I need to pee. Please stop. We've got to find a toilet.'

'But there isn't one near here,' he observes blithely. 'I'm afraid you'll just have to wait.'

'I can't!'

And really I don't think I can much longer, either. Things are getting very serious down there and sweat is pouring off me as I fight to control my water.

He utters another sigh. A big, fake, pantomime sigh this time.

'Very well, then,' he says, as if I were seriously discommoding him somehow, and it's all very tedious. Which, again, is total bullshit, because he's loving every minute of this. He has a special fascination with pissing games, because he knows I once played them with someone else . . .

We get out of the car – very gingerly and awkwardly in my case – and there's the sound of voices somewhere near. And – oh, God! – running water. We must be somewhere near the river, maybe in the vicinity of a country pub or a beauty spot. It's night but there are strollers out and about. People who might see me with my skirt up and my pants down. People who might see me when he makes me do what I've got to do – out here in the open.

I'll just have to take a chance. Not that I've much option. It's either go where he instructs me to or wet myself anyway. If we were in the middle of the Borough Hall car park in broad daylight now, I'd probably have to go. He leads me a little way along what feels like a rough path. Tall stalks of grass brush my legs, and with my knickers around my knees every shuffling uneven step makes me gasp.

'Here,' he says eventually, then, without warning, he swoops down. I feel him pluck at my pants, and I get the message. Feeling as if my eyes are going to pop out beneath my blindfold, I step out of my underwear, moaning with every move or jolt.

I don't know what he does with my knickers, but I suspect that I'm not going to get them back. And I don't care. All I want now is to squat down and let it all go.

But, of course, once I'm down, legs akimbo, I can't. And the multicoloured frustration is so keen I want to wail. Even with the rushing river so close by, I'm all locked up.

'I can't go,' I snivel.

'Oh, poor baby,' he murmurs. 'Poor Miss Lewis. Do you want me to help you?'

Oh, God, yes!

I sense his great presence beside me and, if it wouldn't be so appallingly uncomfortable that I'd probably scream, I'd fall down on my knees and press my lips against his shoes.

He crouches at my side, and once more he slips his hand between my thighs.

And when one long, square-tipped finger works its magic, I do scream. But silently, inside, behind my bitten lip as everything cuts loose and I piss and have an orgasm simultaneously.

This time I don't blank, but seem to experience a moment of total clarity. The sounds around me come into sharp focus. The running water. The echo of my own torrent. The bashing and pounding of my heart. The heavy, broken breathing of the man at my side, who's unable to mask his physical excitement in the execution of one of his own particular perversions. He's wanted to do this ever since I described once being brought off this way by a girlfriend in a transport café.

Silently, as I come down, he hands me tissues to clean myself with, then disposes of them I know not where. I don't feel as if I can speak as we track backwards back to the Toyota. I want to touch him again. Or, more properly, touch him for the first time in the course of this escapade. But somehow I know it's not the time yet.

How long is this bloody road trip going to last?

'Are we there yet?'

We seem to have been driving for hours. Certainly long enough for my inner tension, and my libido, to crank right back up to screaming point again. I clench myself hard around the intrusion in my bottom, imagining that it's Mr Stone's magnificent dick.

'I asked you not to ask that again,' he states, mock coolly.

I pout, hoping the mutinous thrust of my lip will goad him. I know I'm acting bratty, but I also know that's what he wants. This magical mystery tour is turning out to be a pick-and-mix of all his favourite kinks, and there's one more I'd like to add to the selection.

I wait two minutes, then I ask again.

'No. But we soon will be. And you'll regret it, young lady.'

Bingo! He's taken the bait.

Or have I taken his?

The car speeds up, and we twist and turn through the unseen roads and streets. There's passing traffic, so we're probably not in the country or by the river, I guess. I can't see him, and he doesn't speak, but there's a quality to the air that seems to press on my skin. He's as impatient as I am, and, even though he's a past master at disguising his emotions, I know him. And I can read him in the silence and the dark.

We stop, he wrenches on the handbrake, and says, 'We're here. Are you satisfied?'

'No,' I say pertly.

'Well, we'll see about that, then, shall we?'

In far less time than it takes me to grapple clumsily with my seatbelt, he's out of the car, round to the passenger side, and hauling me out on to the pavement, or path, or whatever. He's so much less measured now, so much less in control of himself, and that sense of the balance of power tipping makes my innards flutter dangerously. There's just one more component in our three-for-one special, and, in that, the one who seems to have the least say in the matter is always the one who's really in control.

Together we almost run along a hard surface. I hear the rustle of trees, and sense a boundary of some kind on either side of us. It's a narrow alley. There might be hedges or walls flanking us. There's the snick of a gate, and Mr Stone urges me ahead of him through the opening.

I smile. But I don't let him see it.

'You're an impatient travelling companion, Miss Lewis,' he murmurs, bringing us to a halt. A tree, above and to the side, sighs in agreement. 'Not very restful. Not very soothing.' He pauses, grasps my linked hands, and then presses them against the front of his jeans. 'In fact you could say that your presence on this journey has really wound me up.'

I'll say! He's even more gargantuan than usual.

'What do you think we should do about it?' He does his tango hip swivel when I try to get creative and grope him.

'Discipline me?' I suggest, all innocence, while contemplating another lunge for his equipment.

'Really?' He's holding me at arm's length now. Effortlessly. A man of his size has rather long arms. 'And would you like that?'

Trick question.

'Oh, no ... Please, no ...' I try for piteous and just get pitiful. No need to worry about my Oscar acceptance speech just yet.

'Actually, I think "yes".'

And with that he manhandles me into position over the back of what feels like a conveniently placed wooden chair or seat of some kind. How handy that something just like that should be there.

I dangle, face down – head resting against my shackled arms, thighs taut, bum in the air. Perfectly positioned. And, when he carefully adjusts my skirt, a perfect target. The black flange of the butt plug will make it easier to gauge the distance, no doubt ...

I hear a slow, sliding, insidious sound. And then the snick, snick of a heavy leather belt leaving the loops of his jeans.

Uh-oh! He means business.

I almost shoot out of my skin when he trails it lightly over my naked bottom as if he's allowing me to try the leather on for size. I almost wet myself – again – with longing, when he drapes it in the length of my crease, nudging the plug, the smooth leather dangling against the stickiness of my sex.

'Just three, I think,' he purrs, still teasing me with the object of my correction. 'And I think it would be a good idea if you tried not to cry out.'

Fat chance of that, although I know why he suggests it.

With that he whirls away and I hear his firm tread as he moves into position. I like his purposefulness in these matters. He doesn't waste time with unnecessary taunts and overdramatic Grand Guignol threats. He just gets on with it.

The first blow feels as if I'd been whaled on the right bum cheek by a two-by-four, and my attempt not to make a sound comes out like the squeal of the proverbial stuck pig.

The second feels as if the left side of my arse had been struck by lightning and I make a sound that I don't recognise as human.

The third blow is much lighter, but it catches me right in the crease and knocks the evil-demon butt plug right against the nerves that connect to my clitoris.

I climax violently, shout 'Oh, Bobby!' and pee myself a little.

Afterwards, I turn into a sobbing, blubbering, shuddering, glowing, thankful, soppy mess, and he takes me onto his lap – heedless of my soggy state. I come again, lightly, when he whips out the plug and flings it away into the bushes, and, like a little kitten-girl, I try to kiss his beloved hands, and his dear face, while he unclicks the handcuffs and hurls them away too, after the plug.

Which leaves only the blindfold.

'Are we there yet?' I whisper, managing to get

my lips against his as he reaches for the ribbon that holds the mask in place.

'I think so, baby,' he whispers, returning my kiss as he gives me my sight back.

My lips cling to his for a moment, then I ease away, almost blinded by the nearness of his broad, beloved face.

Then I blink like a baby owl and glance around.

At the chestnut tree. The toolshed. The ironic garden gnomes. Then up towards the bedroom window where there's a soft glow from the bedside lamp he turned on before we set out.

We're here. We're back home again, just where we started from. And I'm so happy because this is where the bed is.

And this time, Clever Bobby, *I'll* do the driving!

Portia Da Costa is a regular author for Black Lace, having written many novels and contributed to numerous short story collections. Her novel, *Suite Seventeen*, is published in June 2007.

Coffee Break Alison Tyler

Café Americano.

Espresso.

Cappuccino.

A shot in the dark.

That last one sounded perfect, because that's what I was doing. Taking a shot in the dark by even being here, standing before the black-and-white marble counter at the upscale café in my office building, staring at the delicately curvy handwritten menu on the chalkboard rather than staring at the gorgeous man less than one foot away. I knew his name by now – Declan. I had picked that up after two weeks of ever so casually hanging around the café far more than I had any business doing. Christ, I'd drunk more cups of coffee than a long-distance trucker during those two weeks, and I was jittery as all hell to prove it. But Declan was worth drinking too much coffee for, worth staying up all night for, worth taking a shot in the dark for.

He had longish blond hair that fell in front of his clear green eyes and a smile that made women – and many men in the equal-opportunities world of Tinseltown – do a double take. He was 22, exactly my age, and he dressed in classic 1950s Hollywood cool: black jeans, black T-shirt, heavily battered motorcycle boots. A wallet chain dangled from his back pocket, and a colourful pin-up girl tattoo peeked out from under his right sleeve.

I didn't think I had a chance with him, and it didn't matter anyway, because I was already taken. Seriously taken. Two years into a relationship taken. Yet that fact didn't stop me from ordering my coffee, from taking too much time to fish out the crisp bills from my red leather wallet just so that I could stand close by him, from holding on to Declan's hand a beat too long when receiving my change.

Being taken didn't keep me from spending all those extra caffeinated-awake hours fantasising about him. I lost my nights to thinking about what it would be like to kiss him, and then moved quickly on to what it might be like to fuck him. Unreal. That was my sense. Simply from the way his mesmerising green eyes watched me when I entered the café, I knew how it would feel to be locked in his embrace. Or better yet, bent over the cool stone countertop waiting for him to slowly lift my pleated skirt, then to gingerly lower my pale-blue panties down my thighs until I was totally exposed. I stroked myself on my old leather sofa while I pictured him fucking me, working his cock between my legs at just the right speed, thrusting inside me while gripping a handful of my long black hair. He would call out my name as he did me. I could hear his voice, memorised now, echoing in my head as my fingertips played over my clit. 'Danielle,' he'd say, 'oh God, Danielle, you feel so good.' I would try to respond, but fail, my voice gone, my face pressed against the cold stone, body held rigid as the climax built inside me. A long line of coffee drinkers would wait for us to be finished so they could grab their morning espressos and be on their way.

Coffee became my number-one aphrodisiac, and in weeks I was an addict. Not just to the coffee bean, but to being near Declan.

'You're back again?' he'd tease when he saw me entering the café each day with my white mug in hand.

'Just can't get enough,' I'd confess, tilting my head as I smiled at him, playing coy as the bitter-strong aroma of coffee hit my nostrils and the sight of him working the machines made me wet. The scent of the coffee bean wasn't supposed to excite me. But it did. Even watching a percolating coffee maker on a TV ad now got me all turned on.

'Well, you always know where to find me . . .'

Sure, I did. He was merely an elevator ride away. I worked in an office upstairs for Jenna Malone, a rich Beverly Hills matron who wrote romance novels in between her various cosmetic procedures. One novel, then an eyelift. A second novel, then lip implants. After her next publication, she was planning a full-body overhaul, one to keep her looking as sexy as the wayward co-eds she wrote into her stories. My job was to run errands in her white convertible BMW and keep her day-planner up to the millisecond.

Oh, yeah, and I also had to pretend to like her books.

Jenna had a philosophy about romance versus reality. In her world, romance could only take place in distant locations: faraway islands or mountain getaways. To her, reality was stark and bland, as unsexy as the thick cigarette-smoke-like smog that hung over Burbank. Maybe this was why she constantly worked to change her appearance, hoping forever to transform herself from reality into something new and sleek. And maybe it was why she never took my opinions seriously. Because, even before I met Declan, it was my belief that romance could happen anywhere. Even in an upscale office building on Doheny Boulevard.

Even in a coffee shop.

In Jenna's office I answered her phone with the same smile as always, but now my smile was all for Declan. During those first few weeks I developed an addict's need. I no longer cared that I couldn't fall asleep before three a.m. The insistent pull within my veins kept me draining my coffee cup just so I had a reason to go downstairs to the café and see him.

Turns out I didn't need a reason. Because soon enough he began coming upstairs to my floor several times a day on the pretence of delivering coffee to other customers in other offices, then dropping a free cup off for me (and one for Jenna, as a cover). There were others in the café who could have done the deliveries; but Declan did it just so he had a reason to come upstairs and see me.

When we realised we both had the same reason for going upstairs and downstairs, we started meeting in the middle, on an empty floor that offered plenty of places to hide. A mega-record company had recently vacated the space in favour of brand-new digs up on the Sunset Strip. Until a new business moved in, the floor was ours, for ten minutes at a time. Declan would push me up against a cool plaster wall and kiss me, and I'd wriggle one hand between our bodies and stroke his hard-on through his chic faded black jeans. I'd work my hand along his shaft, and cup the head in my fist. Then I'd give him a firm squeeze, as if showing him who was boss. As if. By that point I was all his. But I liked to play tough girl.

'God, Danielle,' he'd murmur as I played him through the denim, 'you're going to make me come.'

'That's the idea,' I'd whisper.

'You tease,' he'd say, grabbing me tightly against him, crushing me to him. I could feel his hard, lean body, the muscles in his flat stomach, the strength in his arms. I could feel his cock aligning perfectly with me, so ready, so hard, and that would make me moan.

'Jesus, Danielle,' he'd say, face pressed to my hair, 'you're just a little slut.'

'I'm your coffee slut,' I'd correct him with a laugh, ending our conversation. We had to make the most of every minute, which meant more kissing and fewer words. If Jenna had written our story, she'd have said that our bodies spoke their own language. But that was bullshit. We were simply too busy to talk, lips pressed together, hearts racing. He'd groan when my fingers undid his button-fly so that I could stroke his naked cock, and I'd lean my head back, giving him perfect access to the tender skin at the base of my throat. He'd kiss me there, gently at first, then harder as I pumped him with greater force.

When we parted, I'd return to my office look-ing as flushed and feverish as the pretty but dim heroine in my boss's latest novel. The girl's name was Jacqueline and, of course, she found love in a distant island paradise. But we had similarities nonetheless. I didn't make much of the comparison at the time but, looking back, I definitely fitted the genre. She was young and curious and careless. I was young and curious and careless, as well. I paid attention only to my own desires, and I didn't bother myself with any impending consequences. And there *were* impending consequences.

Plenty of them.

You see, my boyfriend worked in the office, too. Did I mention that? I suppose it's important. In Jenna's novel, Marlon would have been the antagonist – and he definitely did his job at antagonising me, although his presence didn't stop me from roaming, didn't make me hesitate for a moment. In fact, I'll admit that I might have been spurred on a bit by my proximity to danger. Marlon worked at the kidney-shaped white desk across from mine, and he never appeared to be suspicious about my lengthy sojourns downstairs. I may sound proud of the fact, but in reality I'm simply amazed that Declan and I pulled it off for as long as we did.

Marlon was the novelist's assistant, her right-hand man, and he spent hours listening to her read her work aloud, always listening for word repetitions, his greatest pet peeve. Sometimes I would eavesdrop outside the door to Jenna's inner sanctum. I'd hear the two of them debating a word choice, replacing 'caress' with 'stroke' or 'driving' with 'thrusting' or 'petting' with 'rubbing'. Then I'd return to sit breathless at my desk, imagining

Declan doing the things to me that the novelist's characters were doing to each other in their sandy island getaways. Caressing. Stroking. Thrusting. When I could handle it no longer, I'd grab my cup and head downstairs again.

You know. For coffee.

Declan was always ready. Within days of the start of our affair, he'd worked out a deal with his Goth-inspired co-worker. She'd cover his disappearances for him, and he'd let her sneak out early in the evening, or show up late in the morning. She gave me suspicious sidelong glances from under her black-tipped bangs whenever I came in. Or she'd roll her kohl-rimmed eyes and sigh sorrowfully, as if she had all the sadness of a Cure album bottled up inside of her. But she never said a word to me. As soon as I walked through the door, Declan would slide out from behind the counter and head after me to one of our rendezvous spots. Once a new modelling agency took over 'our floor', we retreated to a variety of different locations. Our favourite was a secluded spot behind the building, by the loading docks which were never used. We couldn't have actual sex there, not out in the open, but we made out like high-school kids, which was just as good – at least, for a while.

Declan seemed to know everything I wanted. He'd hold me in place with his hand in my long hair. He'd kiss me until my lips would be bruised when we parted. He'd make me so wet that I took to carrying a spare pair of panties with me in my handbag, knowing that, at some point during the day, I'd need to make a quick change. As soon as he was aware I had extras, Declan began confiscating my dampened pair, promising me that, when he got home that night, he'd come in them. 'Thinking of you,' he told me. 'I wrap those panties around my cock and come so hard, thinking only of fucking you.' That vision made me even wetter than I had been. Would I need to start carrying whole sets of lingerie in my bag, doing multiple changes through-out the day? I sort of liked the idea, emptying my lingerie drawer panty by panty until I had no choice but to go stark naked under my clothes.

'Where were you?' my boyfriend finally asked one afternoon when I returned from an overly long illicit encounter.

'Getting coffee,' I said quickly, before running my tongue along my bottom lip, remembering how it felt to be crushed in Declan's embrace.

Of course, the 'getting coffee' excuse meant that I always had to remember to bring my chipped white porcelain mug with me. To have it filled to the brim before returning to the third-floor office. 'Getting coffee' meant that Declan and I only had about ten minutes to ravish each other, but, as any real romance novelist knows, lovers can do plenty of damage in ten minutes, fantasy island paradise or no. I grew adept at dropping to my knees and undoing his button-fly with my teeth; of drawing out his cock and sucking it with the hungry force of a woman on a mission. And my mission was simple: to make him come. He became knowledgeable at opening my bra with one quick flick of his thumb, of stroking my breasts while telling me exactly what he wanted to do with me when we finally were truly alone. And it didn't take long for us to need to be alone. We moved quickly from foreplay to fucking, and we fucked everywhere we could – in the underground garage, in my car, in the men's room.

While my boyfriend and my boss discussed whether 'sofa' was sexier than 'lounge' and whether 'taunt' was a true synonym for 'tease', Declan and I explored the possibilities of oral sex in an elevator, of putting out in a parking lot, of canoodling in the kitchen. I'd return to the office flushed and damp, but with my full cup of coffee, adrenaline rushing like caffeine through my veins.

Usually, I was the one to head downstairs for a cup of joe. But, when Declan wanted to see me, he still dropped off extra cups of java for us. Jenna thought he had a crush on *her*. 'That coffee boy', she called him. 'He's always bringing me free drinks,' she would say.

Marlon thought it was cute in a pathetic sort of way. 'He must be half your –' he started, then stopped, biting his tongue. Sometimes he wasn't quite as smart as he thought he was or as he pretended to be. 'I mean,' he continued, 'he's just some pretty boy, I'm sure. All fluff and no brains. Nobody who could entertain you.'

But what did Marlon know? His idea of entertaining was spending the afternoon searching for word reps. And he took no notice of my growing addiction. I quickly upped my coffee intake to a record high, explaining my longer absences from the office by a new fascination with the specialty coffees, ones that took slightly longer to prepare. Double expressos and fancy mochas. Anything with whipped cream topping and sprinkles.

'It's good today,' I'd tell Marlon. 'Columbian. Rich and dark. Should I get you a cup?' My hands would be shaking from all the coffee, my heart racing at triple speed, but Marlon never seemed to see. Besides, he liked tea. He even liked to discuss the different types of teas. One for morning, one for mid-afternoon. One as a late-night pick-up. Teas were for the intellectual set, he felt, and Marlon tended to preen about his intellect. He had a Masters, for God's sake, while I was nothing more than a college drop-out. He could give our boss sixteen words for 'sparkling' without resorting to a thesaurus. He made fun of my *Cosmo* subscription, of my occasional California-girl use of 'like' in a sentence, of the fact that I thought making out in a drive-in was hot.

I couldn't give anyone sixteen words for 'sparkling'. After glittering, dazzling and spellbinding, I have to admit that I'm lost. Truthfully, I probably couldn't give anyone sixteen words for *anything*. But I could have told Marlon how Declan had put me up on the cool porcelain edge of the sink in the men's room, of how he'd taken away my panties and spread my thighs so that he could reach my freshly shaved pussy without any barrier. Of how his sweet tongue traced perfect pictures up and over my clit, making ovals and diamonds and figures of eight until my legs shook uncontrollably and I could no longer speak or breathe or think.

Or I could have told Marlon how I'd learned in *Cosmo* the perfect way to go down on a man, fist wrapped tight around the shaft, mouth a magical sucking machine. I could have explained in great detail how I liked to lick my fingertips slowly, while Declan watched, then trick them along his balls, tickling him gently as I sucked him so hard. I could have described how my lipstick smeared all over his skin, leaving rose-pink streaks on his body and my cheeks, and that I was starting to only wear a nude gloss to minimise the retouch factor.

At the very least, I could have told him about how Declan was, like, totally cool, and that the thought of making out with him in a drive-in made my knees weak, while the thought of fucking him in the same drive-in was what made me come each night long after Marlon had gone to sleep. Drinking coffee versus tea started to feel like a reason to fight. What was macho about tea? How could anyone find interest in discussing the merits of oolong over white jasmine? Maybe that was the lack of sleep talking – but even the smell of tea began to repulse me, while I found the very grinds of coffee left in the bottom of my mug to be fascinating remnants destined to turn me on.

Of course, I didn't bother trying to explain any of this to either Marlon or Jenna. They never took my opinions seriously, anyway, even if I was the model reader, exactly the type of chicklet Jenna's publisher catered to. I was the type of girl supposed to dog-ear the pages of her latest tome, living my romantic life vicariously through the escapades of Jacqueline, Jenna's favourite heroine. In reality, it was Jenna who lived her life on the pages. While I lived mine minute by coffee-flavoured minute.

After listening to Jenna and Marlon explain in grave detail that fantasies could only happen in faraway places, with half-dressed native girls and horny sailor boys, I learned about romance versus reality. I learned that fantasies could come true on the vacant second floor of an office building, with a handsome blond man who served coffee and a sultry dark-haired girl who kept having to buy yet another set of pretty panties. The closest *we* got to a sand dune was the gravel in the abandoned dock. The nearest we made it to half-dressed native girls were the models who preened in the atrium between shoots, downing their Diet Cokes and smoking Marlboro Lights.

Declan was everything Marlon was not. My boyfriend, lost in his head, intellectualised everything. Including our sex life. Or lack thereof. And, while Declan might not have possessed a Masters, he had what every romance novel hero has: passion. Electricity. A spark of danger. In fact, the only thing he couldn't offer me was true privacy. All of our meetings were on the sly. Until my boss went away to a writers' conference and Marlon chose to take that same week off to head to the mountains to work on his own writing, an assortment of flavoured teas at his side. This left me and Declan with a room of our own. Or an office, really. A whole office, with a front lobby and two private rooms. Although, truthfully, we didn't really need the whole office. We only needed the rug.

On that very first day, we fucked hard on the floor of the lobby, right in front of my desk. My pink sundress was hiked up to my hips, and my panties were lost somewhere in the corner of the room below the framed covers of the novelist's three books. There were more covers than books because her work had been translated into a variety of languages. So underneath the Dutch version of *Does He Love Me?* lay my twisted pair of petal-pink panties.

Declan kept on his black jeans, and the feel of that faded denim against my naked skin as he ground his body into mine was almost too good to believe. He held me down, held my face in his hands, looked at me with an expression that must have mirrored my own. One that said exactly what I was thinking:

God this is good.

Better than good. It was necessary. We had waited too long for this. We had fucked in every corner of the building, without ever being free to make noise. We had come close to being caught so many times that I'd lost count. Now, we were ready. So ready. His cock was rock hard, and he plunged inside of me with a rhythm that I felt in my own racing heartbeat. He stared into my eyes the whole time, making me tremble with the look on his face. Making me realise how much I wanted to be with him. Not to be with someone who made me feel second best in intelligence and class.

He rotated his hips in small circles as he fucked me, and I reached down between our bodies and slid my fingertips against my clit, pressing hard, gaining the friction I needed to come while he filled me up inside. The climax beat through me, making me beg him for more, for anything, for everything until the waves of pleasure slowly started to subside.

Declan flipped me over and fucked me from behind. I stared at the desk where I worked, at my chipped coffee cup, empty finally since I had no need to keep running downstairs and having it refilled. Then I closed my eyes and let myself feel every sensation. Declan's hands on my waist, holding me steady, his body slamming into mine, slowly and forcefully, rocking me powerfully with every movement. I cried out as he pounded into me, and then I bit into my lip, startled by how loud I'd been. Yet I wanted to be loud. I wanted to make noise. I wanted to be heard.

This was such a long time coming. We'd had to hide for so long. Now, we had room. We had space. We had time. As Declan rocked me, he slid one hand along my waist and then brought his own fingertips between my legs, playing over my still-throbbing clit while continuing to fuck me with that powerhouse force. I groaned and shifted my body, arching back on him. Melding myself to him.

'You like that, don't you?'

Yeah, I liked it. I liked the fact that we weren't pushed up against some wall, or bent over some executive's expensive convertible, or riding up and down in some freight elevator, hoping against hope that the UPS driver wasn't about to make an unexpected delivery. I liked that we were in a large room, with more than enough space around us. And I liked that he didn't have to put his hand over my mouth to muffle the sound of my pleasure, my teeth biting into his fingers to let him know how desperate I was to scream. But all I managed to say was, 'Yes, oh, fuck, yes.'

He understood, and he touched me harder, grazing his short nails against my clit before pinching it between forefinger and thumb. I felt as if I were melting, falling, dissolving into pure pleasure. My body responded to his touch by contracting on his cock tightly, fiercely. We were so in tune, playing off each other, working each other in perfect rhythm.

'Oh yes, you like that,' Declan muttered, his voice low and raw.

He kept touching me, kept fucking me, and I hissed something, some string of nonsense words as I started to come for the second time.

That's precisely when I heard the key in the lock. *Oh, God*, I thought. *Oh, God. Oh, God. Oh, God.* This wasn't a compromising position. There was no compromise involved. This was a flat-out confession.

Jenna, home early for no explainable reason, pushed open the door and strode into the room while Declan and I flew apart from each other in super-speed and tried our best to look as if we hadn't just been fucking doggy-style. Try this yourself sometime. It's not possible. Especially when your dress is hiked up around your hips and your panties are on the floor half the room away from you. It's just not possible to act innocent when your lover's cock is still hard and glistening from your own liquid sex juices and his jeans are open in the centre, as if he's chosen to put himself on display. Yes, his cock was worthy of its own pedestal, but now wasn't the time to unveil the majestic towering force.

My boss stopped, clearly startled to find me away from my desk. And then just as startled to find the coffee-delivery boy in the room with me. She looked at me, looked at Declan, looked at me again, and then headed directly to her office without speaking a word. Yet I thought I caught an expression in her icy-blue eyes as she strode by me. Not one of understanding, though. One of out-and-out jealousy, although her Botox-enhanced brow couldn't furrow to show her displeasure. I was living her words, while all she could do was write them. And have them translated into seventeen languages, including Dutch.

'Oh, God,' Declan said, his thoughts echoing my own from a moment before. 'We're fucked.'

'No –' I couldn't help but smile, because I felt a wave of relief at no longer having to hide '– *I'm* fucked. God, Declan, you fucked me so good.'

Now he grinned too. Marlon would have used a different word there. I knew it. He would have gotten out his red pen, insisting that there was a jarring repetition on the word 'fuck', one that would pull the readers right out of the story. 'You're *screwed*,' he might have said. 'You're *finished*. You're *done*.'

But none of those words rang true to me. And I supposed that was something I'd have to discuss with him when he returned – at least I would right after my next coffee break.

Alison Tyler is the author of numerous Black Lace and Cheek novels. Her short story, *Coffee Break*, appears in the Wicked Words collection, *Sex in the Office*.

Private Performance
Mae Nixon

When Noel Coward said 'It's strange how potent cheap music is,' just for once, I think he got it wrong. Because, when you think about it, all music's pretty potent, isn't it? It can make you feel sad or help you forget your troubles. It sees us through good times and bad and a few bars of a melody can instantly bring to mind a memory you thought you'd buried long ago. I mean, Dvorak's 'New World' Symphony makes everyone think of Hovis, doesn't it? Even people who've never listened to Classic FM still know all the words to 'Everyone's a Fruit and Nutcase' and 'Just one Cornetto'. And, if you've just broken up with your boyfriend, 'I Will Survive' is guaranteed to make you feel better.

Sad, uplifting, poignant or comic, there's a song for every mood and every moment of your life. The other day I heard 'Papa Don't Preach' and was instantly reminded of standing at the edge of the gym at school discos with the smell of polish in my nostrils desperately trying to pretend I didn't mind being a wallflower. And I only have to hear the first line of Sinead O'Connor's 'Nothing Compares 2 U' and I'm fourteen again, slow dancing with Michael Cox at someone's birthday party wondering if he'd kiss me when the song ended and terrified I'd look a fool because he only came up to my chest and I wasn't sure if etiquette demanded I bend down or he stand on tiptoes.

Pavarotti reminds me of sitting at the kitchen table watching my mum cook the Sunday dinner and Ray Charles reminds me of my dad's old 45s. I lost my virginity to Frankie Goes to Hollywood's 'The Power of Love' (1993 re-release) and first said I love you in a noisy pub with Take That's 'Back for Good' playing on the jukebox.

Like it or not, everyone's life has a soundtrack. But, until I met Peter, my personal score had always been delivered by the radio or the CD player or even, when I was a kid, my dad's cherished collection of classic vinyl. Though I've always loved live music, somehow the pivotal moments of my life had always been accompanied by recorded tunes.

There's something unspeakably exciting and miraculous about live music, isn't there? Some extra little frisson of excitement that isn't there when you listen to a recording. All the instruments in the band play their individual parts, yet somehow – almost by magic, it seems to me – they blend together to create music. A complex blend of harmonies and melodies that somehow evoke emotion. Sometimes I'm completely stunned, overwhelmed, by the sheer emotional power of music. Somehow, it seems to enter my soul. It's like good sex: powerful, primal and all consuming. It heightens my senses and makes me feel more alive, more real somehow. I'm serious. The only experience that has ever matched it in intensity is sex. But it had never occurred to me that the two might mix. Until I met Peter...

Usually on a Wednesday night, I got together with two friends for our weekly girls' night in. We took it in turn to play host each week. But this particular evening, neither of them could make it so I'd decided to rent a DVD and pop into the Chinese on the way back. It had been a long day in the shop and I didn't have the energy to cook.

The video shop was quite busy. I squeezed between a middle-aged woman with a small dog on a lead and a young man with a takeaway in a carrier bag. I could smell the spicy aroma of Thai food wafting up at me. It made me feel hungry. I browsed the titles.

'Hello. You don't recognise me, do you?' The man with the takeaway was looking at me.

'I'm afraid not. Should I?'

'I suppose there's no reason why you should. Though I had rather hoped you'd find me at least a bit memorable. I can't tell you how crushing that is for my ego.' He smiled. His eyes were a delicate shade of blue and his blond hair was short and spiky. He seemed slightly familiar, but I couldn't quite place him.

'We've met, I take it?' I struggled to remember.

'At Giovanni's, a couple of weeks ago? I passed your table and you winked at me.'

'Of course. How could I forget? I've still got your phone number in my bag.'

He shrugged his shoulders.

'But you haven't used it.'

'I haven't used it ... yet.'

'How long were you planning on making me wait?'

'You know the rules, I'm sure. Long enough not to seem desperate but soon enough to seem keen.'

'But you intended to call, I hope?' He smiled and crinkles formed around his eyes, making him look playful.

'I hadn't made up my mind, to be honest. But you've saved me the trouble, anyway. And I promise I won't forget you again.'

The woman with the dog stepped back, jostling me. I lost my footing and fell forwards. He put out his hands and steadied me, gripping my upper arms. His hands felt strong and reassuring. Our bodies were not quite touching, my face an inch from his. I could feel his hot breath on my cheek. He released me. The memory of his fingers made me tingle.

'Sorry, what must you think of me? I'm Peter Griffin. Pleased to meet you.' He offered me his hand.

'And I'm Tess Tyler.' We shook hands. His grip was firm, yet friendly. His skin was warm and soft.

'Oh, I know who you are. I've seen you going in and out of your shop in the High Street. In fact I think I was caught in a traffic jam behind your van the other day.'

'You'd better stop there, otherwise I might think you're stalking me.'

'I'm not, I assure you. I'm quite harmless.' His eyes conveyed a mixture of amusement and intensity that made my stomach feel fluttery. His blue eyes sparkled. His mouth was slightly open, his tongue just visible between his teeth. He moistened his lips.

'I'm glad to hear it.' I smiled.

'Are you doing anything this evening?' The timbre of Peter's voice belied the casualness of his request.

'I did have an exciting evening planned with a DVD and a takeaway, but I could change my plans, if there's something more stimulating on offer.'

'Are you hungry?'

'Ravenous.'

'Then I hope you like Thai food.' He held up his takeaway.

'Where do you live?' Much to my surprise, my voice seemed to have grown husky. 'I'm in Park Drive.'

'I live on the corner – you know the old school?'

'Really? I've always wondered what it was like inside. Let's go there, it's nearer.' I took his hand.

Peter's building was a Victorian school that had been converted into apartments in the 1980s. His flat, a former classroom, had high ceilings and plain white walls. One of the walls was composed entirely of windows that started three feet from the floor and finished at the ceiling. It was essentially one long room partitioned at one end to create a separate kitchen and bathroom. Slatted blinds covered the windows, and the floorboards had been sanded to a soft gold colour.

The room had been divided into separate areas. In the centre, there were two sofas, a coffee table and a wide-screen television. At the far end were some bookshelves and an easy chair and some expensive-looking stereo equipment. By the window there was an upright piano and a digital piano.

Peter had divided the takeaway between two plates and poured us each a glass of wine. He had taken off his shoes and sat cross-legged on the floor in front of me. I relaxed back against the sofa, my feet curled under me.

'What do you think of the wine?' He topped up my glass.

'It's good. You have excellent taste.'

'Thanks. I bought it in France last year, direct from the vineyard. It was a real bargain. I've only got half a dozen bottles left now.'

I took another sip of wine.

'Do you play?' I put down my plate and nodded in the direction of the piano.

'Oh, yes. I do it for a living. As a matter of fact, that's why I was in Giovanni's when we met. I was closing a deal with the owner. I'm going to be playing there every Friday night from now on.'

'Really? I'm impressed.'

'It's not as glamorous as it sounds, I assure you. I make my bread and butter as a session musician. Sometimes I spend days and days playing stuff I wouldn't even listen to if I weren't getting paid. I'm building up a bit of a name for myself and there's a record company interested in taking me on, but mostly it's just a job.' Though he was deliberately underplaying his work, I could hear the enthusiasm and dedication in his voice. His eyes glistened.

'I've always envied creative people. I can't even sing.' I smiled.

'But your work is creative, surely? Flower arranging is an art.'

I shook my head. 'It's a technical skill. Anyone can learn it.'

'That can't be true, can it? I mean, you might be able to learn how to choose the right flowers, how to arrange them and what goes with what. But you've got to have an eye for it, haven't you? Flowers are mysterious and magical. Some of them are cheerful and make you want to smile. Others fill you with tenderness at their fragility. Some of them denote sadness and some fill you with passion. You have to understand their innate qualities to make an arrangement really work. And you have to have vision and creativity to even want to do it in the first place. Don't tell me you're not an artist. I simply won't believe it.'

'It's kind of you to say so.'

'Give me your hands.'

'What are you going to do? Read my palm?'

'Give me your hands . . .'

His fingers touched my wrists. He brushed them lightly down the length of my hands all the way to the tips of my fingers. He turned his hands over and held them out to me, palms up. I laid my palms against his. His thumbs caressed the tops of my fingers. I shivered.

'You have the hands of an artist. Look at your long fingers and your shapely nails. And you have a tapering palm. This is the hand of an angel.'

'Yours are beautiful too. So long and sensitive. I should have known you were a pianist. When we shook hands in the video shop I remember thinking how soft they were.' I stroked his fingers.

'That's because I've never done a hard day's work in my life.'

'That's not true, is it? I mean it might not be manual labour but it's hard work, nonetheless. Moving people to tears is a pretty noble occupation.'

'Oh, yes, I do that all the time. Sometimes they throw things as well.'

'Will you play for me?'

'No, I couldn't. I always get nervous and clumsy when someone asks me that.'

'That's must be a bit of a drawback in your job.'

'I don't mind playing in front of a roomful of strangers; that's not personal. But when I have an audience of one I completely forget how to play.'

'I promise I'll stay very quiet. You won't even know I'm here. Please?' I smiled at him.

'Somehow I just don't seem able to say no to you.'

He gave my hands a final squeeze and laid them gently on my knees. He got up and walked over to the piano. He sat down on the bench and closed his eyes. He sat silently for several long moments.

I could hear the murmur of traffic in the street outside. Somewhere in the flat a clock was ticking. Peter's long fingers were poised above the keys. I could see his chest rising and falling. With his eyes closed, his face seemed at once vulnerable and intense. I felt as though he was reaching inside of himself, seeking something secret and personal to share with me as music.

He began to play, eyes still closed. The tinkling notes filled the room. Within a few bars, I recognised the melody. Peter was playing a lilting jazz version of Billie Holiday's 'Lover Man', a piece that I knew well, thanks to my dad's old records. Somehow, he seemed to imbue his playing with the same quality of melancholy and hopefulness that I always heard in Billie's haunting voice.

Peter's body swayed with the music. His hands moved along the keys with ease and precision. I couldn't take my eyes off him. The music seemed to inhabit the room like a separate entity. It seemed palpable and solid. I almost felt as though I could put out my hand and touch it. It sank in through my pores. It crept inside my skull, filling my consciousness with its tenderness and beauty.

His fingers flew along the keyboard. His chest heaved. His parted lips were red and puffy. He was smiling slightly to himself. An expression that I could only describe as bliss transformed his face.

I was on the edge of my seat. The music resonated inside me. I could see that Peter was completely lost in his playing. The sounds his fingers produced were far more than music on a page, learnt by rote and recreated mechanically. He was playing from his heart and guts, allowing his spirit to speak to me through the keys. As he played the final few notes and rested his hands in his lap I noticed that I was holding my breath.

I stood up and walked over to the piano. Peter looked up at me and smiled, uncertain of my reaction.

'Give me your right hand.' My voice was gentle and soft, but my tone left no doubt that I expected to be obeyed. Peter gave me his hand, palm upwards. I received it in the cup of my own left palm, supporting its weight. With my right index finger I traced the outline of his hand. I turned it over, examining it from all angles.

'It's hard to believe that just flesh and blood and bone and sinew can create such beauty.'

Peter smiled his thanks then stood up and led me back over to the sofa. 'You enjoyed my playing?'

'I loved it. You have very talented fingers.'

'And they're versatile too. I also moonlight as a massage therapist.'

'Isn't that just something men say as an excuse to get you naked and oily?'

'No, it's true. Before my playing career took off I earned most of my income that way. You'd be surprised how many musicians have a day job. If you'd like it, I'd be happy to give you a free massage. No strings, strictly professional.' He looked into my eyes and I could see he was being genuine.

'Thanks. I may take you up on that. I get pretty tired sometimes, standing up all day in the shop.' I smiled. Peter topped up my wine glass. 'I really like your flat. It's a lovely space.'

'Yes, I think so too. It's airy and light and, of course, the acoustics are wonderful. But what made me decide to buy it was the garden. It's incredible.'

'What garden? It doesn't have one surely?'

Peter smiled and nodded. 'It's got a very original garden. A very special one. Would you like to see?'

'Why not? I'm intrigued.'

Peter got up and held out his hand to me. I took his hand and he led me across the flat to the front door. He put it on the latch and led me down the corridor outside. At the end of the passage there was a door leading to the roof.

'Do you like it? It used to be the school playground.'

I looked around the roof garden. There was a paved area with pots and troughs full of flowers and a tinkling water feature. To one side, there was a seating area with wooden benches and tables and a barbecue. The garden's perimeter was defined by iron railings. At intervals of about six feet, there was a taller railing which terminated in a spectacular decorated finial. Each pointed tip was surrounded by a complicated cage of wrought iron like a crown.

Peter led me over to the edge of the roof to see the view. The city was spread out like a stage set. The green swathe of Hampstead Heath nestled between the buildings. White headlamps and red tail lights made the roads seem like moving ribbons. In the distance, the skyscrapers of the city rose into the air like modern cathedrals.

It was just growing dusk. The sky was a deep, mysterious blue. I could hear the rumble of traffic. I could feel the breeze on my face. It ruffled my hair. I brushed against one of the pots and the air was instantly filled with the scent of lavender.

I turned to Peter. 'This is beautiful. Breathtaking. Especially at this time of night. It's almost magical.'

Peter nodded. 'You see why I had to buy the flat now. I moved in the week before the millennium. On New Year's Eve I came up here at midnight and watched the fireworks go off. It was an experience I'll never forget.'

I could see the passion and intensity burning in his eyes. He leant against the railing with both hands and looked at the sky. His hair gleamed in the light coming up through the open door. His eyes sparkled. I put my hand on his arm and he turned to look at me. He smiled.

I leant forwards and kissed him, gently. His mouth was soft and warm. He cupped the back of my head in his palm and his other hand stroked my back. I shivered all over.

'It's getting cold. Let's go downstairs.' Peter's voice was soft and tender, his mouth pressed up against my ear.

Downstairs, Peter poured us each another glass of wine. I was feeling pretty relaxed by this time. He was easy to be with: gently amusing and undemanding yet absolutely compelling. As we talked, I noticed he never took his eyes off my face. I stared back, more boldly than I normally would, I admit, but he was making his feelings so clear there didn't seem any point being coy.

I noticed that he had very long, pale lashes and his eyes were an almost lavender blue. He had a way of unconsciously running his tapered fingers through his hair as he talked and I found it totally bewitching. But it was his hands that fascinated me most. Years of piano playing had made them strong and dextrous. He'd obviously spent a lot of time in the sun and the skin on his hands and arms was tanned to a pale golden colour. I could see the muscles and tendons standing out in his forearms and his biceps were nicely shaped: muscular but not over developed. They stretched the sleeves of his white T-shirt ever so slightly and, for some reason, this made me feel protective towards him and in awe of his strength at the same time.

He must have noticed me staring at him because he began to gaze quite openly at my chest and, when I leant forwards to pick up my wine, made a point of trying to look down my front. But it was playful and teasing rather than sleazy; as if he was telling me he found me attractive but was to much of a gentleman to take things further without an invitation.

'That's the third time you've done that, Tess. Does your neck hurt?'

'Done what?'

'You keep rubbing your neck and rolling your head from side to side as if you're in pain.' He demonstrated.

'Yes, I suppose it does ache a bit. It's been a long day and my assistant wasn't in this morning so I had to unload the van all by myself. But it's nothing. I'm sure I'll be all right after a good night's sleep.'

Peter got up and stood behind me. He laid his hands on my shoulders. His palms were warm and heavy. A little shiver of pleasure slid up my spine.

'I'll bet you've had it a while. You've got a way of holding your head on one side, did you know that?'

His hands felt heavenly. I closed my eyes.

'No, I didn't. Maybe you're right. I think I'm just used to it.' His fingers began to knead the muscles of my shoulders. I let out a long, low moan. 'You have magic hands.'

Peter laughed. 'I really am a massage therapist, you know. I'm not just spinning you a line. I used to make a very decent living at it.' His fingers located a sore spot and massaged it.

'Mmmm, that's heavenly. I don't suppose you'd give me a freebie, would you?'

'These days I mostly operate on a barter system.'

'That's very practical, I must say. What would you want in return?'

'I'll leave that up to you. I'm sure you'll find a way of reciprocating.'

'As it happens, I give great reciprocation.'

He leant forwards, cupped my face with both hands and stroked my cheeks with his thumbs.

'I don't doubt it.' He looked up into my eyes.

'But, there's only one problem . . .'

'Yes?'

'You don't appear to have a bed.'

He laughed. 'It's on the mezzanine floor. You have to climb up the ladder.' He pointed.

'It's a long time since I climbed up a ladder to go to bed. Not since my sister and I had bunk beds.'

'You get used to it.' He took my hand and led me over to the ladder. 'Do you want to go first? I'll come up behind you and make sure you don't fall.'

'You can't fool me, you just want to look at my arse.'

'Not just to look. I intend to involve all five of my senses.'

Peter's bed was a futon laid directly on the floor. There was a fluffy white quilt and, a low cupboard at one side of the bed bore a candle, a digital clock and a small CD player. The wall opposite the bed concealed built-in wardrobes behind a panel of mirrors.

'It's nice up here. Sort of peaceful and detached from the rest of the world, somehow. Do you know what I mean?'

Peter nodded. 'I love it, I must admit. It's a very special space.' He stroked my cheek. 'Would you mind if I undressed you now?'

'Is that included in the price?'

'Not officially. In fact, when I was getting paid for it, it tended to be frowned upon. But I'd enjoy it. If you don't mind.' He gazed at me, his eyes shining with need.

'I'm putting myself entirely in your capable hands.'

He untucked my shirt and unbuttoned it with trembling fingers.

'No bra. Now that's a pleasant surprise.' He cupped my breasts and stroked my nipples with his thumbs. They hardened under his touch. His breathing was rapid and loud.

He unzipped my jeans and slid them down.

'And no knickers, either. You're full of surprises.' He got to his knees and pulled my jeans down to my ankles and I stepped out of them. He used his fingertips to trace the curve of my thighs. His fingers moved slowly, exploring every millimetre. His touch was light; his fingers barely brushed my skin. His fingertips were soft and warm. They made me tingle.

He trailed his nails over my buttocks. I shivered all over. He pressed his face against my crotch and inhaled, drinking in my scent. I arched my back and moaned softly.

'Lie down and I'll get my stuff together.'

I lay down on my stomach in the centre of the bed. I felt my body sink into the fluffy white duvet. Peter trotted quietly around the bedroom lighting candles and gathering together the oils he needed for the massage. He selected a disc, slipped it into the CD player and turned it down low. As it began to play I instantly recognised Miles Davis's mellow trumpet.

I relaxed against the bed. I could hear my own breathing, the music and Peter moving quietly around the room. I could hear the ticking clock and, somewhere, in the distance, a police siren.

'I'm just going to get undressed and then I'll be right with you.'

'I didn't realise we both needed to be naked, Peter.' My voice was a husky whisper. 'When I have a massage at the health club, the masseur doesn't undress as well.'

'I haven't got my special white jacket on. I'd get my clothes covered in oil if I kept them on. I'm only concerned about the laundry bills, that's all.' He sat down on the bed beside me and rested an oiled hand on the small of my back. I loved the weight of it, the firm pressure of it against my spine. Peter's skin felt smooth and warm. I closed my eyes and sighed deeply, concentrating on the sensations of his expert hands on my skin.

Peter's fingers slid down my spine in a long, slow *glissando*. I gasped. He massaged the muscles of my back with long, smooth strokes. His hands moved over my skin with the same confidence and accuracy that he had used on the piano.

With gentle pressure he teased out the knots of

tension and soothed them away. His strong fingers worked my stiff shoulders. I felt myself loosening, my muscles softening, the anxiety and pressure of the day dissolving.

He alternated the pressure of fingers: sometimes using just the tips in a teasing *pianissimo* and sometimes putting the weight of his shoulders behind it in a satisfying *fortissimo* that made me gasp in appreciation.

I was drifting away, somewhere on the margin between sleep and consciousness. It was heavenly. The rhythm of Peter's hands on my body, the quiet repetition of the music and the wine I had drunk earlier all combined in a delicious sensation of contentment. I surrendered to it, letting out a soft purr of breath from my throat.

Peter's hands were never still. He played fluttering *arpeggios* along my vertebrae. He tantalised me with deep, slow strokes down the length of my back. I felt the tension building in the base of my belly. I was tingling all over. His hands moved constantly, sliding over the slippery skin. On the downstrokes he slid his palms along my sides, causing his fingers to gently brush the outer curve of my breasts. The slow, sensual caress made me tingle all over.

Peter moved his attention to my lower back and buttocks. He moved each hand in a circular motion up my buttocks towards my back, then down again over my hips. Soon his fingers started to stray along the cleft between my cheeks. On each upstroke he trailed an oiled finger up the crack of my bottom, lingering momentarily over my puckered opening.

I sighed. Peter's fingers began stroking the length of my pussy before swooping upwards and teasing my nether hole. I felt moisture welling inside me and combining with the oil on Peter's probing fingers. My breathing quickened and I unconsciously raised my rear end upwards to meet his moving fingers.

Feathery strokes brought me to a pitch of arousal. I wanted the oily hand to concentrate on my swollen clit, to stay there and stroke it firmly until I came, yet I knew I'd enjoy it all the more if I let Peter take control. I felt torn: half of me wanting to beg for fulfilment, half of me wanting to give myself up to Peter's experienced hands.

I wriggled against the bed and let out a soft moan. 'Oh, you're so cruel,' I said.

Peter laughed. He leant forwards and kissed me tenderly on the shoulder.

Gradually, almost imperceptibly, Peter increased the pressure of his fingers. He slid them along my slippery crack, pausing momentarily to circle the hardened bead of my clit. Then he trailed them upwards between the globes of my bottom, teasing me a little by pressing his thumb against the wrinkled opening.

I opened my thighs wider, offering my pussy to him. The moving fingers were concentrating on the area between my legs now, stroking upwards from my clit to my arsehole. Each stroke was a little firmer than the last and I soon felt the familiar sensations of tension and sensitivity which would lead, inevitably, to orgasm. My clit was hard; my bumhole contracted as the slick fingers teased it. I felt Peter's hand slide under my body and cup my mound. His thumb circled my sensitive clit while his other hand slid rhythmically along my cleft, teasing both holes.

A coil of warmth spread out from my groin. My own moisture mingled with the massage oil and made me slick and slippery. Peter's fingers stroked my clit rhythmically and firmly.

Sweat filmed my body. Damp hair clung to my face in wild tendrils. My eyes fluttered under closed lids. My pulse beat in my throat. My hands clutched handfuls of duvet as Peter fingers coaxed me to a crescendo. I began to moan softly.

I was on the edge now, riding the line between arousal and orgasm. I let out a sharp cry as two of Peter's fingers entered me, quickly followed by two into my arse.

My body began to shudder. I gripped the duvet, my taut body racked with pleasure.

'Peter! Oh, Peter!' I screamed. My thighs quivered. My clit twitched and throbbed under his expert hands. I was coming. Peter pushed his fingers deeper into both my holes, intensifying the delicious sensations.

I never wanted it to end but, gradually, my muscles began to relax. My cunt stopped throbbing and my breathing returned to normal. I wiped my unruly hair away from my forehead and turned to smile at him.

'I bet you got a lot of tips, when you were doing it for a living.'

'I didn't go quite this far in those days. Let's just say that I put in a few extras just for you.' He stroked my back, running the flat of his hand down my spine.

'If I remember correctly, I promised you some reciprocation.'

'Only if you feel like it.'

I pushed Peter back down onto the bed. I rolled on top of him and kissed him. He tasted of wine. I nibbled on his plump lower lip. My nostrils were filled with the scent of arousal. I could feel his heart beating against my chest. I kissed his neck, concentrating on the sensitive spot near the ear. I nibbled. Peter's body stiffened under me. He tilted his hips and pressed his groin against me.

'Patience,' I murmured before moving on to lick the base of his throat. I trailed my tongue over smooth, scented skin. I nuzzled into Peter's hairy armpits, drinking in his essence. I kissed my way across his chest, seeking out a nipple. I teased the hardened bud with the tip of my tongue, barely touching it. I bathed it with saliva then blew on it, causing it to peak and contract even more. Peter let out a low moan.

I loved the way his nipples swelled and reddened when I excited them. I sucked one into my mouth and flicked it with my tongue; feasting on it. I swapped sides and treated the other nipple to the same loving attention.

A red flush of arousal coloured Peter's chest and throat. Sweat made his skin shine. His breathing was thready and rapid. I reached down and started to stroke the length of his torso with my fingertips, feather-light strokes, barely making contact with his sensitised skin. Peter's skin formed into goose pimples in response. I trailed my fingers down his sides. Starting at the armpits, I ran them down as far as the hips, then up again over the belly and chest. I could tell that he ached to have his cock touched. He wriggled his hips, begging to feel my touch. I shook my head.

I continued my exploration of Peter's body. I stroked up and down his chest, my fingers gentle and soft, still barely touching. Gradually I moved nearer and nearer to his hardened nipples. I circled them with my fingertips, knowing how tantalising this must feel. Then I used my thumbs to brush across the swollen buds. Peter moaned with delight.

I slid down his body and positioned myself between his parted legs. Peter was obviously a natural blond. He had a mat of golden pubes which he kept trimmed. His balls were tight with excitement, his scrotum already thickened and taut.

The tip of his cock was wet and glistening. The light from the candle seemed to make the slippery moisture glow. I inhaled deeply, filling my nostrils with the delicious perfume of man. I used my thumbs to stroke around Peter's balls, then slid down to tease his bumhole.

'Suck me, please,' begged Peter urgently.

I dipped my head and extended my tongue. I pushed it against Peter's helmet and explored him with it. I loved the sensation of my mouth against the silky skin of his cock.

Peter spread his legs wider and thrust his crotch at me.

I tongued his helmet, at the same time fingering his bumhole. Every so often I pushed my fingertip against the sensitive opening. Peter was gasping and writhing beneath me. I knew he wanted me to start sucking him, but I wasn't ready yet. I wanted to work him up to a peak of arousal, make him beg for it.

'Please!' Peter was practically wailing.

I took no notice, but began licking at his helmet. I gripped the base of his cock and squeezed. Peter let out a soft moan and his thighs started to tremble.

'OK,' I said, 'I know what you want.'

I opened my mouth and took him inside. I sucked hard and Peter shivered with delight. I flicked his helmet with my tongue, squirming it into the hole.

The next track on the CD began and I instantly recognised 'My Funny Valentine'. Peter moaned as my mouth made contact. I knew it wouldn't take long for him to come now; he was so aroused. I closed my eyes and relished the sensation of slick, hot cock against my own slippery mouth. I eagerly sucked on his rigid member. His musky man smell filled my nostrils as my nose nuzzled against his pubes. Miles Davis's swooping trumpet solo seemed the perfect soundtrack for this moment. Its dancing cadence somehow seemed to echo the rhythm of arousal, layering and building until the inevitable moment of crescendo.

I sucked hard. Peter started thrashing his limbs and thrust his cock hard into my mouth. I slid my lips up and down his shaft, allowing his cock to fuck my mouth. The trumpet sang urgently.

Peter was moaning and panting now, one hand on the back of my head. I could feel his thigh muscles tensing. I sucked hard, every so often squeezing his cock firmly with my hand. I slid a finger inside his tight arsehole.

The repetitive base beat pounded in rhythm with Peter's excited breathing. His hips rocked to a tempo of their own, grinding his crotch against my eager face. I sucked harder, at the same time circling my finger inside him.

Peter was groaning and mumbling. I felt his thighs trembling, taut with tension. I knew he was close to coming and I quickened the pace and intensity of my sucking. I slid a second finger into his arse and rotated them firmly. The trumpet's restless melody resonated inside me, echoing my own need and Peter's excitement.

My slick lips slid along Peter's shaft. His bottom raised off the bed as he ground his cock against my face.

The song built towards its frenzied, exultant coda. Peter started moaning, shouting almost; meaningless sounds which signalled his orgasm. I held on, struggling to keep my mouth in place as he came. Hot spunk spread over my tongue and I swallowed, relishing its thick saltiness. I sucked hard, coaxing the last aftershocks of orgasm from him as the last note of the song died out.

Finally, Peter stopped shouting and I slid my fingers out of his bum. I placed one last kiss on his cock and rested my head on his belly.

Fifteen minutes later, we had an encore and since then Peter and I have played plenty of duets together. Sometimes we go for classical, creating symphonies with separate movements and themes, and sometimes we opt for jazz with its raw rhythms and energy. Occasionally, we even do solos, one of us performing while the other plays audience.

A week later I watched him receive a standing ovation after his first performance at Giovanni's. I joined in the applause knowing that I alone would be getting a private performance later on.

Mae Nixon's short stories have appeared in numerous Words collections.

Beautiful Things Cal Jago

I have always loved beautiful things: exquisitely crafted pieces of jewellery; elegantly cut cloth forming tailoring perfection; the awe-inspiring works of fine art that hang in galleries and the homes of the wealthy. Yes, beautiful things are an important part of my life. Just as important though, is the process by which they come to be mine.

My life is divided fairly equally between my small but successful PR firm in Oxford, my bright and spacious modern loft apartment just outside the city centre and, my favourite environment of all, shops. Fashion boutiques, shoe shops, jewellers, book stores – all of these, amongst others, have the ability to send my pulse rocketing. Because, as much as I try to control these urges that I have, the emotional and physical responses provoked by a shopping trip are simply unparalleled. Retailers are my salvation. It is a simple fact: for me, few things beat the thrill of acquiring new things.

I know that, for some, the credit card is the Holy Grail but I'm a cash kind of girl. Crude, some may say. But somehow, for me, cash lacks the quiet desperation of 'slapping it on the plastic'. And besides, beautiful things deserve crisp notes being counted into a perfectly manicured hand.

And so it was that one afternoon, after a

particularly fraught time with one of my more demanding clients, I found myself standing on a pavement looking through the window of Serendipity, a jeweller's that had caused quite a stir when it had opened six months before. In fact, 'jeweller's' doesn't seem the right word; that somehow implies fusty, traditional and endless rows of diamonds and yellow gold. Serendipity wasn't like that at all. The owner was a thirty-something designer who, with a flourish of metals and stones, had brought a quirky coolness to accessorising the discerning women in the town. The pieces on sale were largely one-offs made by the owner herself although some of them were bought in from an array of exotic locations. They were unique, striking, beautiful. Expensive, of course, but isn't it worth it to have something so exceptional? I had perused a few times before and had even bought a couple of items – an unusual turquoise pendant and an armful of silver bangles, which chimed as I moved. But this time, before I'd even entered the shop, I knew that things were different. This time I was after something very special.

The owner looked up and smiled as I entered. She didn't look so much arty as businesslike. Like me, she wore an impeccably cut suit; classic black, the jacket tailored tightly around her narrow waist, its hem flared over the curve of her hips which, in turn, were hugged by flattering bootcut trousers. Her blonde hair, however, was piled up on her head, held in place with a mass of pins. It was a laissez-faire look, totally befitting an artist, the technique for which I had never quite mastered with my own long dark hair.

A young woman stood towards the back of the shop trying on a selection of silver rings. They were pretty much the only items openly on display which could easily be handled as most of the merchandise was locked in cases. She sighed heavily as she tried on the rings and then rejected them, looking around to see whether anything else caught her eye.

I wandered through the shop inspecting the jewellery, taking in countless exquisite items. I imagined how the pieces would feel displayed on my body: fine, delicate chains grazing my collarbone, heavy pendants nudging insistently at my cleavage, chunky metallic bracelets and chokers gripping my flesh, their coldness pressed against my fevered skin.

I stopped abruptly as my gaze settled on a strand of perfectly formed golden moonstones. At certain angles the spheres appeared almost translucent yet the next moment, from a slightly different position, a spectacular amber sheen was visible as an inner glow that seemed almost to float across the convex surface.

Breathtaking.

I forced myself to look away and caught the owner's eye, gesturing towards the cabinet.

'You'd like a closer look?' she asked, stepping towards the glass.

I nodded. 'Please.' I felt my voice waiver as I spoke and cleared my throat.

She removed the object of my desire from its

glass prison and draped it across her hand, suspending the necklace in front of my face.

'So beautiful,' I whispered, reaching out to touch one of the perfect stones. It felt cool against the heat of my fingertips. 'May I?'

She smiled, seemingly pleased that I had the good taste to recognise its flawlessness. 'Of course. They're stunning, aren't they? I brought them back from Burma and then set them in the silver. It's so difficult to find good, pure examples of even the blue moonstones over here, let alone these golden ones. They're so rare. And so lovely.'

I smiled and nodded and felt a little light-headed as I took the necklace from her and marvelled at the weight of it. Holding it in one hand, I moved the fingers of my other hand across the stones, gently gliding my skin over each sphere one by one. I closed my eyes as I caressed them, my fingertips lingering on their cold smoothness. I felt my skin prickle and had to stop myself from actually gasping. All the signs were there; this was the one. This was perfect.

The girl trying on the rings sighed dramatically. 'Do you have any smaller ones?' she asked.

The owner frowned slightly. 'There are all sorts of sizes there,' she said. 'You might just have to try a few, I'm afraid, until you find one that fits.'

The girl sighed again and pouted. 'I've been trying them,' she said, sulkily. 'Have you got any more out the back?'

The owner forced a smile, turning away from me slightly so that she could keep an eye on her. 'What sort of thing were you after?'

'Not sure.' She smiled sweetly. 'But I'm sure I'll know it when I see it so if you could bring anything else out ...'

The owner edged towards the young woman, suspicion furrowing her brow. She looked from me to her; me, a professional thirty year-old in a smart suit carrying a briefcase, her, the sullen, slightly scruffy teenager who just seemed out of place in such a shop. Her gaze settled again on me. Placing the necklace gently on top of a display cabinet beside me, I smiled sympathetically and rolled my eyes. 'It's fine, I'm not in any hurry,' I assured her.

The owner returned my smile, relieved. 'I'm sure we can find you something,' she said firmly and immediately moved to the teenager's side, mentally trying to account for every bit of stock she had so much as looked at. Which was perfect actually because, as soon as she left me, I silently scooped the necklace into my palm and nudged it with my fingertips, forcing it a little way up the sleeve of my jacket. Then I placed my hand in my trouser pocket.

OK, yes, I know what I said before about the thrill of counting crisp banknotes into a manicured hand and so on and that still stands true. I really do enjoy spending. But, for me, shopping trips don't always entail expenditure. Sometimes, my desire to simply take is just too overwhelming and the thrill I get from that is deeper and more potent than watching a cash register eat my money as a sales assistant asks me whether I want to keep the hangers.

My heart thumped. I stood still for a moment and tried to regain my poise. If you truly wish to go undetected, even after you have left the shop, you obviously cannot show any physical sign of guilt. This includes bolting from the premises at the first possible opportunity. I glanced at the owner, checking that I hadn't been spotted. What would happen, I wondered, if she had seen what I'd done?

I imagined the grip of her hand on my wrist as she stopped me from walking away with my precious pickings. When she had spoken to me about the necklace, her voice had been low, throaty, authoritative. Would she still sound so in control when, digging her fingers harder into my flesh, she would accuse me of theft?

'I saw you,' she would insist, her face just inches from mine.

I would simply smile as her hand dived, determined, into my pocket. She would frown, perplexed, as she rummaged around and then come up empty-handed. Then she'd plunge it in again, forcing it down, down into the depths of my silk-lined pockets, her fingers slipping on the smooth, shiny material and sliding down a new route, surprising her with their sudden misdirection. The beauty of customised clothing; concealed pockets. Her smooth palm would roam across my bare thigh tops and I would hold my breath until her fingers located what she wanted.

'It's one of my little idiosyncrasies,' she would say quietly, her fingers moving ever higher up my legs, the stones of the necklace trailing cold across my skin. 'As a businesswoman, I'm quite keen for people to pay for what they take.'

I would hesitate, trying to ignore the exact location of her hand whilst determining the best course of action. Her cool measured stare would confirm that remorse was probably a wise option.

'OK,' I'd say, doing my best to look genuinely devastated by my bad behaviour, 'I'm sorry. Of course I'll pay.'

She'd smile. 'Yes, you most certainly will.'

And then she'd spin me around, flip me over the display cabinet, raise my skirt unceremoniously, and mete out a just punishment until I truly repented and orgasmically vowed to mend my klepto ways.

I shook my head, forcing myself to return to reality. Whilst the very real danger of getting caught is always there and adds an irresistible frisson to proceedings, I can think of nothing more humiliating than the fall-out of being found out. The reality would not, after all, be a sensual spanking from a sexy blonde but bad coffee in a police interview room, a trip to the magistrates court followed by a couple of column inches in the local paper, and a fine, imprisonment or both. But actually, if I'm being honest, the thing which makes me baulk most at being captured isn't the humiliation, the punishment, the inevitable criminal record. It's the fact that, if I end up in the shit, it would mean that I wasn't any good. It would signal absolute failure on my part as a thief. And that simply isn't true.

I forced myself to focus. The owner looked bored with the girl now. She had tried her best to find her something but the young woman appeared to have lost interest. I anticipated their exchange would shortly come to an end so decided it was time to make my move.

Suddenly, the shop door flew open and a man entered looking flushed and out of breath. All three of us immediately turned to look at him, so forceful was his entrance.

'If anyone owns that silver Audi outside, you'd better go and move it,' he panted. 'You're about to get a parking ticket.'

'Shit.' I looked at the owner, startled. 'Two seconds,' I said, waving a random two fingers in the air. I dashed out of the shop before she had time to speak, slowed down only by bumping into the man who, by now, was having a full-on rant about traffic wardens.

Almost before I knew it I was out on the pavement. Perfect. I marched quickly as the blood rushed in my head and white noise roared in my ears. As every inch of my skin buzzed and a familiar tingle crept the length of my body, a wide smile stretched across my face.

My first act of retail deviance was when, aged seven, I slipped a miniature bottle of perfume into my new grown-up handbag in the local chemist's. It was a pretty, shapely bottle, you see, and I wanted to look at it again at home. So I took it. It made sense to me to do that but, of course, I knew it was wrong. I'd held my breath to the point of giddiness as I left the shop, convinced that I was going to be caught. I was terrified but exhilarated as I galloped along the high street and then home feeling ready to burst. And it was a thrill which lasted for the hours I sat in my bedroom with the door firmly closed, touching the glass and admiring the way the light caught its contours. Actually, it was a thrill that never really went away.

I have stolen ever since. I love the sheer excitement of it; the rush I get from palming the item, feigning nonchalance and then racing home with my newly acquired treasure. It is something which, once experienced, I was never going to stop. Some steals are more exciting than others, depending on the item or the circumstances or my mood, but there's always some sort of thrill to be had.

I've stolen lots of things over the years, obviously: silk scarves, cashmere gloves, lingerie, jewellery, leather goods, books, hosiery ... And perfume, because old habits die hard. Expensive things. Beautiful things. Never the usual bars of chocolate and lipsticks, even when I was a teenager. The items always have to be worth it. It's not about me being a snob or having to steal what I can't afford. Things simply have to be expensive because it adds to the excitement – and the beauty. And because I take what is expensive and beautiful I do not steal for the sake of it. I haven't got cupboards full of unwanted rubbish at home; stuff I don't like or want but couldn't, nevertheless, resist taking. Consequently, I have a real fondness for all the items I have taken. One of my favourites, without a doubt, is the shoe.

The shoe was magnificent, the ultimate, classic black stiletto. A simple, unadorned, iconic shape; the mere sight of it made me swoon. I took it to the sullen sales assistant who duly lumbered out the back to hunt it down. When she finally returned, it was to tell me, in a flat voice, that it was one half of the only pair left in the shop. A size five, it was too small for my long slender feet. I was distraught but decided not to be defeated. In spite of it being the wrong size it was, in all respects, the perfect shoe. It was beautiful. So I wordlessly took it from where it hung off the tips of two of her fingers, held my head high and carried it out of the shop. No one tried to stop me. Who, after all, would be expecting a customer to walk out holding one lone, ill-fitting stolen shoe? Often, it's all about confidence. Confidence, attitude and, sometimes, the element of surprise. For the past three years it has enjoyed pride of place on top of the bookcase beside my bed and, at the risk of sounding dramatic, I shall actually be a very happy woman if it's the last thing I see before I go to sleep every night for the rest of my life.

No matter what I've stolen and in what circumstances the after-effect is always the same. It is excitement, but not just the excitement of getting away with a crime. This excitement is far beyond that and it is the driving force that keeps me going back to steal time and time again. The moment of theft is potent and heady. But what comes afterwards absolutely blows my mind.

I have lost count of the number of times my journey home from a steal has been interrupted simply because I could not wait. In my car, in public loos, in a rickety lift in a multi-storey car park, even in the stairwell at the bottom of my apartment building because my front door a few flights up just seemed like a million miles away; time and time again, hot and wet, I have hurriedly, impatiently triggered the release I so desperately sought. And when I can wait, I can't wait for long. Once through the front door, my beautiful steals clasped in my hand, clothes are shed and my fingers create all that I have thought about from the moment I had walked into the shop and spotted my object of desire. Not that the action that succeeds the steal is always solo. On the contrary, there is sometimes a whole new dimension to proceedings.

My heart wasn't all that thumped on my journey from the jeweller's to home. I had passed countless department stores, cafés and pubs, all of which I could have used for instant relief. But I was determined to wait. My hands shook as I rammed the key into my front door. Images from the scenes in the shop flashed through my mind at speed as I quickly stepped out of my shoes and began to unbutton my jacket: the young woman looking every inch the common shoplifter as she surreptitiously toyed with the rings; the knowing glances the owner and I shared as she fell for my act, convinced that I was the one she should trust; the man's flustered intrusion making my escape so flawless; my initial glimpse of the perfect strand of moonstones and the first time my fingertips touched their coolness. My breathing quickened at my recollections as I entered my bedroom. It was no good. I couldn't wait.

Without wasting another second, I made my way to the bed, kneeling one knee on the edge of the mattress whilst keeping the other foot firmly planted on the floor for balance's sake. I briefly looked up at the huge ornate mirror that rose from behind the wrought-iron headboard. The mirror had been a steal too although, obviously, it wasn't easily slipped into a pocket or dropped into a handbag. It had taken a lot of careful planning, that mirror. But it had been worth it to own something so decadently beautiful. The reflection that stared back at me now was flushed; from collarbones up across throat to cheeks, my skin glowed. One hand slid down the front of my trousers as I half-stood and half-crouched while the other reached forwards to steady myself on the bed. My legs were splayed slightly, completing an image that was positively whorish. I smiled and closed my eyes as my fingers skimmed over my underwear for the briefest moment.

'Caught you red-handed.'

I froze.

A soft, teasing laugh then from someone who knew me too well; someone who knew how impatient I could be at such times.

'It was all your talk of traffic wardens back there.' I straightened up and turned to smile over one shoulder at him. 'It just turned me on,' I continued lightly.

He laughed again. 'It worked though, didn't it?'

I giggled as he came to stand behind me, his hands gently circling my waist. 'Mmm, absolutely.'

One of his hands travelled downwards, stroking the swell of my hip and over my thigh. 'Another job well done, wouldn't you say?' He lifted up the back of my hair and softly kissed my neck. My skin prickled. I was so ready.

'Don't make me wait any longer,' I whispered.

He tutted. 'So impatient.'

'Mmm ... So ...'

'So ...?'

I sighed but couldn't help smiling. 'So ... don't make me wait any longer.'

'What is it you want?' he asked maddeningly.

I rolled my eyes. 'You know what.'

'Tell me.'

I sighed again and he must have felt sorry for me. Well, either that or he was as eager as I was. I felt movement behind me.

'Turn around,' he said and I did as I was told.

We stood facing each other. I held my breath as, grinning, he produced the moonstone necklace from his pocket.

He held his hand aloft, the necklace dangling from his fingers. Fingers which, less than an hour before, had deftly entered my pocket and lifted the stones in the split second before I had strode from the shop. To anyone else his intrusion would have been imperceptible. But not to me.

'An excellent choice,' he said.

I laughed. 'Would you expect anything less of me?'

I reached out to touch the stones but he quickly jerked his wrist, flicking the necklace out of my reach. I frowned.

'Take off your clothes.'

After six years together, that phrase still had such power. Alex, my soulmate, playmate and sometime-partner-in-crime, never tired of watching me strip. He didn't want anything showy. He just wanted me to slowly and deliberately remove each item of clothing until I stood naked before him. He could, he said quite charmingly, see something new and feel some element of surprise every time he saw me undress. I did as instructed, maintaining eye contact with him as each garment was shed.

He nudged one of his knees into mine, pushing me backwards onto the bed. Straddling my thighs, he bent his head as though to kiss me but his mouth hovered no more than an inch above mine. Then, with most of the necklace scooped into the palm of his hand, he held one of the stones between his thumb and forefinger and gently moved it across my lower lip. Its coolness felt almost wet as it glided across my sensitive skin. I exhaled softly as he moved it more insistently and then pressed gently but firmly, forcing my lips apart and allowing the stone, and the fingers that held it, to enter my mouth.

'It really was an excellent choice,' he said again. 'So beautiful, isn't it?'

I nodded in silence.

He released some more of the strand and it cascaded over my chin and throat. I felt the stone inside my mouth touch my tongue, Alex's finger and thumb sliding further between my lips after it. I closed my teeth around the golden sphere, gently grazing Alex's flesh. He quickly removed his hand and the moonstone and shimmied his body further down the bed, his jean-clad lower half making room for itself between my legs.

He reached forwards and trailed the necklace lower. I felt its weight slither down my neck as the stones bumped along my collarbones. He steered them lower, lower, and I closed my eyes feeling them nestle into my cleavage. I felt his fingertips on me then, brushing lightly against my skin as he carefully arranged the necklace over my body. I marvelled at how restrained he could be, how patient, when I knew he was as desperate as I was. I squirmed a little as I felt him shifting the stones around one of my breasts. He rolled one of the stones across the nipple and I bit gently on my lower lip as I felt myself stiffen under his touch.

Suddenly, he drew both ends of the necklace together, pulling them tight and ensnaring my nipple between the hardness of two neighbouring stones. I gasped, surprised by the unexpected movement and the brief burn of pain which accompanied it. The intensity of the heat began to disperse as Alex's tongue began to lap at the buzzing flesh.

I held my breath as his tongue skimmed down my ribcage, lingering over my stomach and then continuing its travels down towards my navel. With my eyes tightly shut, I focused on the incredible feeling and tried to resist the temptation to thrust my hips off the bed towards him. Knowing Alex, if I looked too impatient, he would make me wait even longer before giving me what I wanted. I tensed as I felt a sharp blast of breath between my legs and sunk my fingers into Alex's hair as it brushed inside my thigh. Finally, he had stopped toying with me.

Alex didn't quite make the contact I was expecting, however. Instead, one by one, he began to press the stones inside me. His fingers forced them deeper while, every so often, he tugged gently on the strand provoking exquisite sensations inside me. Full of the stones and his fingers, my heart pounded between my thighs. Each stone and finger moved deliciously, probing, twisting and pushing against my insides. The pressure was so immensely pleasurable it became almost unbearable. I reached for his wrist and grabbed it tightly, not knowing whether to force his hand deeper or push it away. Highly skilled at prolonging agonising ecstasy, Alex was perfectly capable of keeping me there on the brink all night. But, fortunately for me and my impatient ways, he was not so cruel that afternoon. A low moan escaped from deep in my throat as he began to remove the necklace from me. The dragging friction created inside as he pulled each one free caught my breath as my muscles involuntarily contracted around them, trying to keep them from leaving.

Kneeling, he grabbed my slender ankles and eased my legs above his shoulders. The muscles in my calves and thighs stretched taut as he found the angle he wanted. It was the position I wanted too; suddenly and unhappily empty, I ached for the fullness I had just experienced. He grappled with his belt. Once free he was inside me, deep, within seconds. He remained perfectly still for a moment and then, with remarkable self-restraint, he began to move oh so slowly. He drove into me with long smooth strokes and I wriggled beneath him wishing that I could have half the self-control he had.

'Harder,' I said. 'Please.'

He bent down and kissed me, his tongue pushing deep into my mouth and sliding across my teeth while he nipped and tugged at my lips. I grabbed the back of his head, pressing his mouth harder to mine but he reached for my hand and pulled it away from him. In a moment he had coiled the necklace around one wrist and now jerked it downwards, pinning my left arm above my head on the mattress. I gasped in surprise as his free hand secured my other wrist just as securely under his weight. A burst of air broke from my lungs as he stretched forwards and began to tongue my wrist – an erogenous zone I have never fully understood and can often forget about but one which, when remembered, gets me every time. I writhed beneath him, his tongue circling the sensitive spot and sliding across the moonstones which had, just a few minutes before, been buried deep within my core.

'I can taste you,' he murmured and his thrusts quickened.

I dug my heels into his shoulders and pushed my hips towards him to meet his force. As I heard his teeth clatter against the stones and, just an instant later, felt them close around the sensitive flesh of my wrist, my whole being seemed to spasm as ripple upon ripple of pleasure rushed over me. Seconds later, Alex's body went rigid and he shouted out close to my ear as he flooded me with heat.

It took a few minutes to come down from my orgasmic high and bring reality back into focus. We lay curled on our sides, Alex behind me, his chest pressed against my back, his knees nestled behind mine. He absently trailed a finger along my shoulder making my nipples tighten once more. I sighed, utterly sated. My body hummed; my mind felt totally serene.

'What are you thinking about?' Alex asked.

I smiled into my pillow and trailed my fingertips over the necklace which lay on the bed beside me. 'Nothing much,' I said.

But, as always, he knew me too well. His toes nudged at mine beneath the duvet.

'Well...' I wriggled onto my other side and smiled sweetly. 'As it happens, I did see a rather lovely print in that little art shop on my way home. A female nude actually,' I said watching Alex's eyes light up. 'I think it would look perfect in here,' I continued, already trying to picture the layout of the shop and a potential escape route. 'So I think –' I paused to kiss him lightly on the lips '– I might just have to treat myself.'

Cal Jago's short stories have appeared in numerous Wicked Words collections.